THE BLACK SWAN

Thomas Mann

THE BLACK SWAN

Translated from the German by

WILLARD R. TRASK

Alfred A. Knopf   *New York*
1964

L. C. catalog card number: 54-7197

THIS IS A BORZOI BOOK,
PUBLISHED BY ALFRED A. KNOPF, INC.

Published June 7, 1954
Reprinted, December 1964

Originally published in German as DIE BETROGENE, *copyright
1953 by Thomas Mann*

THE BLACK SWAN

I N THE twenties of our century a certain Frau
Rosalie von Tümmler, a widow for over a dec-
ade, was living in Düsseldorf on the Rhine, with
her daughter Anna and her son Eduard, in comfortable if not luxurious circumstances. Her husband, Lieutenant-Colonel von Tümmler, had lost
his life at the very beginning of the war, not in
battle, but in a perfectly senseless automobile ac-
cident, yet still, one could say, "on the field of
honour"—a hard blow, borne with patriotic resignation by his wife, who, then just turned forty,
was deprived not only of a father for her children, but, for herself, of a cheerful husband,
whose rather frequent strayings from the strict
code of conjugal fidelity had been only the symptom of a superabundant vitality.

A Rhinelander by ancestry and in dialect, Rosalie had spent the twenty years of her marriage in the busy industrial city of Duisburg, where von Tümmler was stationed; but after the loss of her husband she had moved, with her eighteen-year-old daughter and her little son, who was some twelve years younger than his sister, to Düsseldorf, partly for the sake of the beautiful parks that are such a feature of the city (for Frau von Tümmler was a great lover of Nature), partly because Anna, a serious girl, had a bent for painting and wanted to attend the celebrated Academy of Art. For the past ten years, then, the little family had lived in a quiet linden-bordered street of villas, named after Peter von Cornelius, where they occupied the modest house which, surrounded by a garden and equipped with rather outmoded but comfortable furniture dating from the time of Rosalie's marriage, was often hospitably opened to a small circle of relatives and friends—among them professors from the Academies of Art and Medicine, together with a married couple or two from the world of industry —for evening gatherings which, though always decorous in their merriment, tended, as the Rhineland custom is, to be a little bibulous.

Frau von Tümmler was sociable by nature. She loved to go out and, within the limits possible to her, to keep open house. Her simplicity and cheerfulness, her warm heart, of which her love for Nature was an expression, made her generally liked. Small in stature, but with a well-preserved figure, with hair which, though now decidedly grey, was abundant and wavy, with delicate if somewhat aging hands, the backs of which the passage of years had discoloured with freckle-like spots that were far too many and far too large (a symptom to counteract which no medication has yet been discovered), she produced an impression of youth by virtue of a pair of fine, animated brown eyes, precisely the colour of husked chestnuts, which shone out of a womanly and winning face composed of the most pleasant features. Her nose had a slight tendency to redden, especially in company, when she grew animated; but this she tried to correct by a touch of powder—unnecessarily, for the general opinion held that it became her charmingly.

Born in the spring, a child of May, Rosalie had celebrated her fiftieth birthday, with her children and ten or twelve friends of the house, both ladies and gentlemen, at a flower-strewn table in an inn garden, under the particoloured light of Chinese lanterns and to the chime of glasses raised in fervent or playful toasts, and had been gay with the general gaiety—not quite without effort: for some time now, and notably on that evening, her health had been affected by certain critical organic phenomena of her time of life, the extinction of her physical womanhood, to whose spasmodic progress she responded with repeated psychological resistance. It induced states of anxiety, emotional unrest, headaches, days of depression, and an irritability which, even on that festive evening, had made some of the humorous discourses that the gentlemen had delivered in her honour seem insufferably stupid. She had exchanged glances tinged with desperation with her daughter, who, as she knew, required no predisposition beyond her habitual intolerance to find this sort of punch-inspired humour imbecilic.

She was on extremely affectionate and confidential terms with this daughter, who, so much older than her son, had become a friend with whom she maintained no taciturn reserve even in regard to the symptoms of her state of transition. Anna, now twenty-nine and soon to be thirty, had remained unmarried, a situation which was not unwelcome to Rosalie, for, on purely selfish grounds, she preferred keeping her daughter as her household companion and the partner of her life to resigning her to a husband. Taller than her mother, Fräulein von Tümmler had the same chestnut-coloured eyes—and yet not the same, for they lacked the naïve animation of her mother's, their expression was thoughtful and cool. Anna had been born with a clubfoot, which, after an operation in her childhood that produced no permanent improvement, had always excluded her from dancing and sports and indeed from all participation in the activities and life of the young. An unusual intelligence, a native endowment fortified by her deformity, had to compensate for what she was obliged to forgo. With only two or three hours of private tutoring a day, she had easily got through school and passed her final examinations, but had then ceased to pursue any branch of academic learning, turning instead to the fine arts, first to sculpture, then to painting, in which, even as a student, she had struck out on a course of the most extreme intellectualism, which, disdaining mere imitation of nature, transfigured sensory content into the strictly cerebral, the abstractly symbolical, often into the cubistically mathematical. It was with dismayed respect that Frau von Tümmler looked at her daughter's paintings, in which the highly civilized joined with the primitive, the decorative with profound intellection, an extremely subtle feeling for colour combinations with a sparse asceticism of style.

"Significant, undoubtedly significant, my dear child," she said. "Professor Zumsteg will think highly of it. He has confirmed you in this style of painting and he has the eye and the understanding for it. One has to have the eye and the understanding for it. What do you call it?"

"Trees in Evening Wind."

"Ah, that gives a hint of what you were intending. Are those cones and circles against the greyish-yellow background meant to represent trees—and that peculiar spiralling line the wind? Interesting, Anna, interesting. But, heavens above, child! adorable Nature—what you do to her! If only you would let your art offer something to the emotions just once—paint something for the heart, a beautiful floral still life, a fresh spray of lilac, so true to life that one would think one smelt its ravishing perfume, and a pair of delicate Meissen porcelain figures beside the vase, a gentleman blowing kisses to a lady, and with everything reflected in the gleaming, polished table-top . . ."

"Stop, stop, Mama! You certainly have an extravagant imagination. But no one can paint that way any more!"

"Anna, you don't mean to tell me that, with your talent, you can't paint something like that, something to refresh the heart!"

"You misunderstand me, Mama! It's not a question of whether I can. Nobody can. The state of the times and of art no longer permits it."

"So much the more regrettable for the times

and art! No, forgive me, child, I did not mean to say quite that. If it is life and progress that make it impossible, there is no room for regret. On the contrary, it would be regrettable to fall behind. I understand that perfectly. And I understand too that it takes genius to think up such an expressive line as this one of yours. It doesn't express anything to me, but I can see beyond doubt that it is extremely expressive."

Anna kissed her mother, holding her palette and wet brush well away from her. And Rosalie kissed her too, glad in her heart that her daughter found in her work—which, if abstract and, as it seemed to her, deadening, was still an active handicraft—found in her artist's smock comfort and compensation for much that she was forced to renounce.

৶

How greatly a limping gait curtails any sensual appreciation, on the part of the opposite sex, for a girl as such, Fräulein von Tümmler had learned early, and had armed herself against the fact with a pride which (in turn, as these things go), in cases where a young man was prepared despite her deformity to harbour an inclination toward her, discouraged it through coldly aloof disbelief and nipped it in the bud. Once, just after their change of residence, she had loved—and had been grievously ashamed of her passion, for its object had been the physical beauty of the young man, a chemist by training, who, considering it wise to turn science into money as rapidly as possible, had, soon after attaining his doctorate, manœuvred himself into an important and lucrative position in a Düsseldorf chemical factory. His swarthy, masculine handsomeness, together with an openness of nature which appealed to men too, and the proficiency and application which he had demonstrated, aroused the enthusiasm of all the girls and matrons in Düsseldorf society, the young and the old being equally in raptures over him; and it had been Anna's contemptible fate to languish where all languished, to find herself condemned by her senses to a universal feeling, confronted with whose depth she struggled in vain to keep her self-respect.

Dr. Brünner (such was the paragon's name), precisely because he knew himself to be practical

and ambitious, entertained a certain corrective
inclination toward higher and more recondite
things, and for a time openly sought out Fräulein
von Tümmler, talked with her, when they met
in society, of literature and art, tuned his insin-
uating voice to a whisper to make mockingly
derogatory remarks to her concerning one or another of his adorers, and seemed to want to con-
clude an alliance with her against the mediocri-
ties, who, refined by no deformity, importuned
him with improper advances. What her own
state was, and what an agonizing happiness he
aroused in her by his mockery of other women
—of that he seemed to have no inkling, but only
to be seeking and finding protection, in her in-
telligent companionship, from the hardships of
the amorous persecution whose victim he was,
and to be courting her esteem just because he
valued it. The temptation to accord it to him
had been strong and profound for Anna, though
she knew that, if she did, it would only be in an
attempt to extenuate her weakness for his masculine attraction. To her sweet terror, his assiduity
had begun to resemble a real wooing, a choice

and a proposal; and even now Anna could not but admit that she would helplessly have married him if he had ever come to the point of speaking out. But the decisive word was never uttered. His ambition for higher things had not sufficed to make him disregard her physical defect nor yet her modest dowry. He had soon detached himself from her and married the wealthy daughter of a manufacturer, to whose native city of Bochum, and to a position in her father's chemical enterprise there, he had then betaken himself, to the sorrow of the female society of Düsseldorf and to Anna's relief.

Rosalie knew of her daughter's painful experience, and would have known of it even if the latter, at the time, in a moment of uncontrollable effusion, had not wept bitter tears on her mother's bosom over what she called her shame. Frau von Tümmler, though not particularly clever in other respects, had an unusually acute perception, not malicious but purely a matter of sympathy, in respect to everything that makes up the existence of a woman, psychologically and physiologically, to all that Nature has inflicted upon woman; so that in her circle hardly an event or circumstance in this category escaped her. From a supposedly unnoticed and private smile, a blush, or a brightening of the eyes, she knew what girl was captivated by what young man, and she confided her discoveries to her daughter, who was quite unaware of such things and had very little wish to be made aware of them. Instinctively, now to her pleasure, now to her regret, Rosalie knew whether a woman found satisfaction in her marriage or failed to find it. She infallibly diagnosed a pregnancy in its very earliest stage, and on these occasions, doubtless because she was concerned with something so joyously natural, she would drop into dialect—"*Da is wat am kommen*," she would say, meaning "something's on the way." It pleased her to see that Anna ungrudgingly helped her younger brother, who was well along in secondary school, with his homework; for, by virtue of a psychological shrewdness as naïve as it was keen, she divined the satisfaction that the superiority implied by this service to the male sex brought to the jilted girl.

It cannot be said that Rosalie took any particular interest in her son, a tall, lanky redheaded boy, who looked like his dead father and who, furthermore, seemed to have little talent for humanistic studies, but instead dreamed of building bridges and highways and wanted to be an engineer. A cool friendliness, expressed only perfunctorily, and principally for form's sake, was all that she offered him. But she clung to her daughter, her only real friend. In view of Anna's reserve, the relation of confidence between them might have been described as one-sided, were it not that the mother simply knew everything about her repressed child's emotional life, had known the proud and bitter resignation her soul harboured, and from that knowledge had derived the right and the duty to communicate herself with equal openness.

In so doing, she accepted, with imperturbable good humour, many a fondly indulgent or sadly ironical or even somewhat pained smile from her daughter and confidante, and, herself kindly, was glad when she was kindly treated, ready to laugh at her own simple-heartedness, convinced that

it was happy and right—so that, if she laughed at
herself, she laughed too at Anna's wry expression. It happened quite often—especially when
she gave the reins to her fervour for Nature, to
which she was forever trying to win over the
intellectual girl. Words cannot express how she
loved the spring, *her* season, in which she had
been born, and which, she insisted, had always
brought her, in a quite personal way, mysterious
currents of health, of joy in life. When birds
called in the new mild air, her face became radi-
ant. In the garden, the first crocus and daffodil,
the hyacinths and tulips sprouting and flaunting
in the beds around the house, rejoiced the good
soul to tears. The darling violets along country
roads, the gold of flowering broom and forsythia,
the red and the white hawthorns—above all, the
lilac, and the way the chestnuts lighted their
candles, white and red—her daughter had to admire it all with her and share her ecstasy. Rosalie
fetched her from the north room that had been
made into a studio for her, dragged her from her
abstract handicraft; and with a willing smile
Anna took off her smock and accompanied her

mother for hours together; for she was a surprisingly good walker and if in company she concealed her limp by the utmost possible economy of movement, when she was free and could stump along as she pleased, her endurance was remarkable.

The season of flowering trees, when the roads became poetic, when the dear familiar landscape of their walks clothed itself in charming, white and rosy promise of fruit—what a bewitching time! From the flower catkins of the tall white poplars bordering the watercourse along which they often strolled, pollen sifted down on them like snow, drove with the breeze, covered the ground; and Rosalie, in raptures again, knew enough botany to tell her daughter that poplars are "diœcious," each plant bearing only flowers of one sex, some male, others female. She discoursed happily on wind pollination—or, rather, on Zephyrus' loving service to the children of Flora, his obliging conveyance of pollen to the chastely awaiting female stigma—a method of fertilization which she considered particularly charming.

The rose season was utter bliss to her. She raised the Queen of Flowers on standards in her garden, solicitously protected it, by the indicated means, from devouring insects; and always, as long as the glory endured, bunches of duly refreshed roses stood on the whatnots and little tables in her boudoir—budding, half-blown, full-blown—especially red roses (she did not favour the white), of her own raising or attentive gifts from visitors of her own sex who were aware of her passion. She could bury her face, eyes closed, in such a bunch of roses and, when after a long time she raised it again, she would swear that it was the perfume of the gods; when Psyche bent, lamp in hand, over sleeping Cupid, surely his breath, his curls and cheeks, had filled her sweet little nose with this scent; it was the aroma of heaven, and she had no doubt that, as blessed spirits there above, we should breathe the odour of roses for all eternity. Then we shall very soon, was Anna's sceptical comment, grow so used to it that we simply shan't smell it any more. But Frau von Tümmler reprimanded her for assuming a wisdom beyond her years: if one was bent on scoffing, such an argument could apply to the whole state of beatitude, but joy was none the less joy for being unconscious. This was one of the occasions on which Anna gave her mother a kiss of tender indulgence and reconciliation, and then they laughed together.

Rosalie never used manufactured scents or perfumes, with the single exception of a touch of Eau de Cologne from Farina's on the Jülichsplatz. But whatever Nature offers to gratify our sense of smell—sweetness, aromatic bitterness, even heady and oppressive scents—she loved beyond measure, and absorbed it deeply, thankfully, with the most sensual fervour. On one of their walks there was a declivity, a long depression in the ground, a shallow gorge, the bottom of which was thickly overgrown with jasmine and alder bushes, from which, on warm, humid days in June with a threat of thundershowers, fuming clouds of heated odour welled up almost stupefyingly. Anna, though it was likely to give her a headache, had to accompany her mother there time and again. Rosalie breathed in the heavy, surging vapour with delighted relish, stopped, walked on, lingered again, bent over the slope, and sighed: "Child, child, how wonderful! It is the breath of Nature—it is!—her sweet, living breath, sun-warmed and drenched with moisture, deliciously wafted to us from her breast. Let us enjoy it with reverence, for we too are her children."

"At least you are, Mama," said Anna, taking the enthusiast's arm and drawing her along at her limping pace. "She's not so fond of me, and she gives me this pressure in my temples with her concoction of odours."

"Yes, because you are against her," answered Rosalie, "and pay no homage to her with your talent, but want to set yourself above her through it, turn her into a mere theme for the intellect, as you pride yourself on doing, and transpose your sense perceptions into heaven knows what —into frigidity. I respect it, Anna; but if I were in Mother Nature's place, I should be as offended with all of you young painters for it as she is." And she seriously proposed to her that if she was set upon transposition and absolutely must be abstract, she should try, at least once, to express odours in colour.

This idea came to her late in June, when the lindens were in flower—again for her the one lovely time of year, when for a week or two the avenues of trees outside filled the whole house, through the open windows, with the indescribably pure and mild, enchanting odour of their late bloom, and the smile of rapture never faded from Rosalie's lips. It was then that she said: "That is what you painters should paint, try your artistry on that! You don't want to banish Nature from art entirely; actually, you always start from her in your abstractions, and you need something sensory in order to intellectualize it. Now, odour, if I may say so, is sensory and abstract at the same time, we don't see it, it speaks to us ethereally. And it ought to fascinate you to convey an invisible felicity to the sense of sight, on which, after all, the art of painting rests. Try it! What do you painters have palettes for? Mix bliss on them and put it on canvas as chromatic joy, and then label it 'Odour of Lindens,' so that people who look at it will know what you were trying to do."

"Dearest Mama, you are astonishing!" Fräulein von Tümmler answered. "You think up problems that no painting teacher would ever dream of! But don't you realize that you are an incorrigible romanticist with your synæsthetic mixture of the senses and your mystical transformation of odours into colours?"

"I know—I deserve your erudite mockery."

"No, you don't—not any kind of mockery," said Anna fervently.

৪৵

Yet on a walk they took one afternoon in mid-August, on a very hot day, something strange befell them, something that had a suggestion of mockery. Strolling along between fields and the edge of a wood, they suddenly noticed an odour of musk, at first almost imperceptibly faint, then stronger. It was Rosalie who first sniffed it and expressed her awareness by an "Oh! Where does that come from?" but her daughter soon had to concur: Yes, there was some sort of odour, and, yes, it did seem to be definable as musky—there was no doubt about it. Two steps sufficed to bring them within sight of its source, which was repellent. It was there by the roadside, seething in the sun, with blowflies covering it and flying all around it—a little mound of excrement, which they preferred not to investigate more closely. The small area represent a meeting-ground of animal, or perhaps human, fæces with some sort of putrid vegetation, and the greatly decomposed body of some small woodland creature seemed to be present too. In short, nothing could be nastier than the teeming little mound; but its evil effluvium, which drew the blowflies by hundreds, was, in its ambivalence, no longer to be called a stench but must undoubtedly be pronounced the odour of musk.

"Let us go," the ladies said simultaneously, and Anna, dragging her foot along all the more vigorously as they started off, clung to her mother's arm. For a time they were silent, as if each had to digest the strange impression for herself. Then Rosalie said:

"That explains it—I never did like musk, and I don't understand how anyone can use it as a perfume. Civet, I think, is in the same category. Flowers never smell like that, but in natural-history class we were taught that many animals secrete it from certain glands—rats, cats, the civet-cat, the muskdeer. In Schiller's *Kabale und Liebe*—I'm sure you must remember it—there's a little fellow, some sort of a toady, an absolute fool, and the stage direction says that he comes on screeching and spreads an odour of musk through the whole parterre. How that passage always made me laugh!"

And they brightened up. Rosalie was still capable of the old warm laughter that came bubbling from her heart—even at this period when the difficult organic adjustments of her time of life, the spasmodic withering and disintegration of her womanhood, were troubling her physically and psychologically. Nature had given her a friend in those days, quite close to home, in a corner of the Palace Garden ("Paintbox" Street was the way there). It was an old, solitary oak tree, gnarled and stunted, with its roots partly exposed, and a squat trunk, divided at a moderate height into thick knotty branches, which themselves ramified into knotty offshoots. The trunk was hollow here and there and had been filled with cement—the Park Department did something for the gallant centenarian; but many of the branches had died and, no longer producing leaves, clawed, crooked and bare, into the sky; others, only a scattered few but on up to the crown, still broke into verdure each spring with the jaggedly lobed leaves, which have always been considered sacred and from which the victor's crown is twined. Rosalie was only too pleased to see it—about the time of her birthday she followed the budding, sprouting, and unfolding of the oak's foliage on those of its branches and twigs to which life still forced its way, her sympathetic interest continuing from day to day. Quite close to the tree, on the edge of the lawn in which it stood, there was a bench; Rosalie sat down on it with Anna, and said:

"Good old fellow! Can you look at him without being touched, Anna—the way he stands there and keeps it up? Look at those roots, woody, and thick as your arm, how broadly they clasp the earth and anchor themselves in the nourishing soil. He has weathered many a storm and will survive many more. No danger of his falling down! Hollow, cemented, no longer able to produce a full crown of leaves—but when his time comes, the sap still rises in him—not everywhere, but he manages to display a little green, and people respect it and indulge him for his courage. Do you see that thin little shoot up there with its leaf-buds nodding in the wind? All around it things haven't gone as they should, but the little twig saves the day."

"Indeed, Mama, it gives cause for respect, as you say," answered Anna. "But if you don't mind, I'd rather go home now. I am having pains."

"Pains? Is it your—but of course, dear child, how could I have forgotten! I reproach myself for having brought you with me. Here I am staring at the old tree and not worrying about your sitting there bent over. Forgive me. Take my arm and we will go."

From the first, Fräulein von Tümmler had suffered severe abdominal pains in advance of her periods—it was nothing in itself, it was merely, as even the doctors had put it, a constitutional infliction that had to be accepted. Hence, on the short walk home, her mother could talk about it to the suffering girl soothingly and comfortingly, with well-intentioned cheerfulness, and indeed —and particularly—with envy.

"Do you remember," she said, "it was like this the very first time, when you were still just a young thing and it happened to you and you were so frightened, but I explained to you that it was only natural and necessary and something to be glad over and that it was really a sort of day of glory because it showed that you had finally ripened into a woman? You have pains beforehand—it's a trial, I know, and not strictly necessary, I never had any; but it happens; aside from you, I know of two or three cases where there are pains, and I think to myself: Pains, *à la bonne heure!*—for us women, pains are something different from what they are elsewhere in Nature and for men; they don't have any, except when they're sick, and then they carry on terribly, even Tümmler did that, your father, as soon as he had a pain anywhere, even though he was an officer and died the death of a hero. Our sex behaves differently about it; it takes pain more patiently, we are the long-suffering, born for pain, so to speak. Because, above all, we know the natural and healthy pain, the God-ordained and sacred pain of childbirth, which is something absolutely peculiar to woman, something men are spared, or denied. Men—the fools!—are horrified, to be sure, by our half-unconscious screaming, and reproach themselves and clasp their heads in their hands; and, for all that we scream, we are really laughing at them. When I brought you into the world, Anna, it was very bad. From the first pain it lasted thirty-six hours, and Tümmler ran around the apartment the whole time with his head in his hands, but despite everything it was a great festival of life, and I wasn't screaming myself, *it* was screaming, it was a sacred ecstasy of pain. With Eduard, later, it wasn't half so bad, but it would still have been more than enough for a man—our lords and masters would certainly want no part in it. Pains, you see, are usually the danger-signals by which Nature, always benignant, warns that a disease is develop-

ing in the body—look sharp there, it means, something's wrong, do something about it quick, not
so much against the pain as against what the pain
indicates. With us it can be like that too, and
have that meaning, of course. But, as you know
yourself, your abdominal pain before your periods doesn't have that meaning, it doesn't warn
you of anything. It's a sport among the species of
women's pains and as such it is honourable, that
is how you must take it, as a vital function in the
life of a woman. Always, so long as we are that—
a woman, no longer a child and not yet an in-
capacitated old crone—always, over and over,
there is an intensified welling up of the blood of
life in our organ of motherhood, by which precious Nature prepares it to receive the fertilized
egg, and if one is present, as, after all, even in my
long life, was the case only twice and with a long
interval between, then our monthly doesn't
come, and we are pregnant. Heavens, what a joyous surprise when it stopped the first time for me,
thirty years ago! It was you, my dear child, with
whom I was blessed, and I still remember how I
confided it to Tümmler and, blushing, laid my

face against his and said, very softly: 'Robert, it's happened, all the signs point that way, and it's my turn now, *da is wat am kommen.* . . .'"

"Dearest Mama, please just do me the favour of not using dialect, it irritates me at the moment."

"Oh, forgive me, darling—to irritate you now is the last thing I meant to do. It's only that, in my blissful confusion, I really did say that to Tümmler. And then—we are talking about natural things, aren't we?—and, to my mind, Nature and dialect go together somehow, as Nature and the people go together—if I'm talking nonsense, correct me, you are so much cleverer than I am. Yes, you are clever, and, as an artist, you are not on the best of terms with Nature but insist on transposing her into concepts, into cubes and spirals, and, since we're speaking of things going together, I rather wonder if they don't go together too, your proud, intellectual attitude toward Nature, and the way she singles you out and sends you pains at your periods."

"But, Mama," said Anna, and could not help laughing, "you scold me for being intellectual, and then propound absolutely unwarrantable intellectual theories yourself!"

"If I can divert you a little with it, child, the most naïve theory is good enough for me. But what I was saying about women's natural pains I mean perfectly seriously, it should comfort you. Simply be happy and proud that, at thirty, you are in the full power of your blood. Believe me, I would gladly put up with any kind of abdominal pains if it were still with me as it is with you. But unfortunately that is over for me, it has been growing more and more scanty and irregular, and for the last two months it hasn't happened at all. Ah, it has ceased to be with me after the manner of women, as the Bible says, in refererence to Sarah, I think—yes, it was Sarah, and then a miracle of fruitfulness was worked in her, but that's only one of those edifying stories, I suppose—that sort of thing doesn't happen any more today. When it has ceased to be with us after the manner of women, we are no longer women at all, but only the dried-up husk of a woman, worn out, useless, cast out of nature. My dear child, it is very bitter. With men, I believe, it usually doesn't stop as long as they are alive. I know some who at eighty still can't let a woman alone, and Tümmler, your father, was like that too—how I had to pretend not to see things even when he was a lieutenant-colonel! What is fifty for a man? Provided he has a little temperament, fifty comes nowhere near stopping him from playing the lover, and many a man with greying temples still makes conquests even among young girls. But we, take it all in all, are given just thirty-five years to be women in our life and our blood, to be complete human beings, and when we are fifty, we are superannuated, our capacity to breed expires, and, in Nature's eyes, we are nothing but old rubbish!"

To these bitter words of acquiescence in the ways of Nature, Anna did not answer as many women would doubtless, and justifiably, have answered. She said:

"How you talk, Mama, and how you revile and seem to want to reject the dignity that falls to the elderly woman when she has fulfilled her life, and Nature, which you love after all, translates her to a new, mellow condition, an honourable and more lovable condition, in which she still can give and be so much, both to her family and to those less close to her. You say you envy men because their sex life is less strictly limited than a woman's. But I doubt if that is really anything to be respected, if it is a reason for envying them; and in any case all civilized peoples have always rendered the most exquisite honours to the matron, have even regarded her as sacred— and we mean to regard you as sacred in the dignity of your dear and charming old age."

"Darling"—and Rosalie drew her daughter close as they walked along—"you speak so beautifully and intelligently and well, despite your pains, for which I was trying to comfort you, and now you are comforting your foolish mother in her unworthy tribulations. But the dignity, and the resignation, are very hard, my dear child, it is very hard even for the body to find itself in its new situation, that alone is torment enough. And when there are heart and mind besides, which would still rather not hear too much of dignity and the honourable estate of a matron, and rebel against the drying up of the body— that is when it really begins to be hard. The soul's adjustment to the new constitution of the body is the hardest thing of all."

"Of course, Mama, I understand that very well. But consider: body and soul are one; the psychological is no less a part of Nature than the physical; Nature takes in the psychological too, and you needn't be afraid that your psyche can long remain out of harmony with the natural change in your body. You must regard the psychological as only an emanation of the physical; and if the poor soul thinks that she is saddled with the all too difficult task of adjusting herself to the body's changed life, she will soon see that she really has nothing to do but let the body have its way and do its work on herself too. For it is the body that moulds the soul, in accordance with its own condition."

Fräulein von Tümmler had her reasons for saying this, because, about the time that her mother made the above confidence to her, a new face, an additional face, was very often to be

seen at home, and the potentially embarrassing developments which were under way had not escaped Anna's silent, apprehensive observation.
ॐ
The new face—which Anna found distressingly commonplace, anything but distinguished by intelligence—belonged to a young man named Ken Keaton, an American of about twenty-four whom the war had brought over and who had been staying in the city for some time, giving English lessons in one household or another or simply commandeered for English conversation (in exchange for a suitable fee) by the wives of rich industrialists. Eduard had heard of these activities toward Easter of his last year in school and had earnestly begged his mother to have Mr. Keaton teach him the rudiments of English a few afternoons a week. For though his school offered him a quantity of Greek and Latin, and fortunately a sufficiency of mathematics as well, it offered no English, which, after all, seemed highly important for his future goal. As soon as, one way or another, he had got through all those boring humanities, he wanted to attend the Poly-

technic Institute and after that, so he planned, go to England for further study or perhaps straight to the El Dorado of technology, the United States. So he was happy and grateful when, respecting his clarity and firmness of purpose, his mother readily acceded to his wish; and his work with Keaton, Mondays, Wednesdays and Saturdays, gave him great satisfaction—because it served his purpose, of course, but then too because it was fun to learn a new language right from the rudiments, like an abecedarian, beginning with a little primer: words, their often outlandish orthography, their most extraordinary pronunciation, which Ken, forming his l's even deeper down in his throat than the Rhinelanders and letting his r's sound from his gums unrolled, would illustrate with such drawn-out exaggeration that he seemed to be trying to make fun of his own mother tongue. "Scrr-ew the top on!" he said. "I sllept like a top." "Alfred is a tennis play-err. His shoulders are thirty inches brr-oaoadd." Eduard could laugh, through the whole hour and a half of the lesson, at Alfred, the broad-shouldered tennis player, in whose praise so much was said with the greatest possible use of "though" and "thought" and "taught" and "tough," but he made very good progress, just because Ken, not being a learned pedagogue, used a free and easy method—in other words, improvised on whatever the moment brought and, hammering away regardless, through patter, slang, and nonsense, initiated his willing pupil into his own easy-going, humorous, efficient vernacular.

Frau von Tümmler, attracted by the jollity that pervaded Eduard's room, sometimes looked in on the young people and took some part in their profitable fun, laughed heartily with them over "Alfred, the tennis play-err," and found a certain resemblance between him and her son's young tutor, particularly in the matter of his shoulders, for Ken's too were splendidly broad. He had, moreover, thick blond hair, a not particularly handsome though not unpleasant, guilelessly friendly boyish face, to which in these surroundings, however, a slight Anglo-Saxon cast of features lent a touch of the unusual; that he was remarkably well built was apparent despite his loose, rather full clothes; with his long legs and narrow hips, he produced an impression of youthful strength. He had very nice hands, too, with a not too elaborate ring on the left. His simple, perfectly unconstrained yet not rude manner, his comical German, which became as undeniably English-sounding in his mouth as the scraps of French and Italian that he knew (for he had visited several European countries)—all this Rosalie found very pleasant; his great natural-ness in particular prepossessed her in his favour; and now and again, and finally almost regularly, she invited him to stay for dinner after Eduard's lesson, whether she had been present at it or not. In part her interest in him was due to her having heard that he was very successful with women. With this in mind, she studied him and found the rumour not incomprehensible, though it was not quite to her taste when, having to eructate a little at table, he would put his hand over his mouth and say "Pardon me!"—which was meant for good manners, but which, after all, drew at-tention to the occurrence quite unnecessarily.

Ken, as he told them over dinner, had been

born in a small town in one of the Eastern states, where his father had followed various occupations—broker, manager of a gas station—from time to time too he had made some money in the real-estate business. Ken had attended high school, where, if he was to be believed, one learned nothing at all—"by European standards," as he respectfully added—after which, without giving the matter much thought, but merely with the idea of learning something more, he had entered a college in Detroit, Michigan, where he had earned his tuition by the work of his hands, as dishwasher, cook, waiter, campus gardener. Frau von Tümmler asked him how, through all that, he had managed to keep such white, one might say aristocratic, hands, and he answered that, when doing rough work, he had always worn gloves—only a short-sleeved polo shirt, or nothing at all from the waist up, but always gloves. Most workmen, or at least many of them —construction workers, for example—did that back home, to avoid getting horny proletarian hands, and they had hands like a lawyer's clerk, with a ring.

Rosalie praised the custom, but Keaton differed. Custom? The word was too good for it, you couldn't call it a "custom," in the sense of the old European folk customs (he habitually said "Continental" for "European"). Such an old German folk custom, for example, as the "rod of life"—village lads gathering fresh birch and willow rods at Christmas or Easter and striking ("peppering" or "slashing," they called it) the girls, and sometimes cattle and trees, with them to bring health and fertility—that was a "custom," an age-old one, and it delighted him. When the peppering or slashing took place in spring, it was called "Smack Easter."

The Tümmlers had never heard of Smack Easter and were surprised at Ken's knowledge of folklore. Eduard laughed at the "rod of life," Anna made a face, and only Rosalie, in perfect agreement with their guest, showed herself delighted. Anyhow, he said, it was something very different from wearing gloves at work, and you could look a long time before you found anything of the sort in America, if only because there were no villages there and the farmers were

not farmers at all but entrepreneurs like everyone else and had no "customs." In general, despite being so unmistakably American in his en-
tire manner and attitude, he displayed very little
attachment to his great country. He "didn't care
for America"; indeed, with its pursuit of the
dollar and insensate church-going, its worship of
success and its colossal mediocrity, but, above
all, its lack of historical atmosphere, he found it
really appalling. Of course, it had a history, but
that wasn't "history," it was simply a short, boring "success story." Certainly, aside from its
enormous deserts, it had beautiful and magnificent landscapes, but there was "nothing behind
them," while in Europe there was so much behind everything, particularly behind the cities,
with their deep historical perspectives. American
cities—he "didn't care for them." They were put
up yesterday and might just as well be taken
away tomorrow. The small ones were stupid
holes, one looking exactly like another, and the
big ones were horrible, inflated monstrosities,
with museums full of bought-up European cul-
tural treasures. Bought, of course, was better

than stolen, but not *much* better, for, in certain places things dating from A.D. 1400 and 1200 were as good as stolen.

Ken's irreverent chatter aroused laughter; they took him to task for it too, but he answered that what made him speak as he did was precisely reverence, specifically a respect for perspective and atmosphere. Very early dates, A.D. 1100, 700, were his passion and his hobby, and at college he had always been best at history—at history and at athletics. He had long been drawn to Europe, where early dates were at home, and certainly, even without the war, he would have worked his way across, as a sailor or dishwasher, simply to breathe historical air. But the war had come at just the right moment for him; in 1917 he had immediately enlisted in the army, and all through his training he had been afraid that the war might end before it brought him across to Europe. But he had made it—almost at the last minute he had sailed to France, jammed into a troop transport, and had even got into some real fighting, near Compiègne, from which he had carried away a wound, and not a slight one, so that he had had to lie in hospital for weeks. It had been a kidney wound, and only one of his kidneys really worked now, but that was quite enough. However, he said, smiling, he was, in a manner of speaking, disabled, and he drew a small disability pension, which was worth more to him than the lost kidney.

There was certainly nothing of the disabled veteran about him, Frau von Tümmler observed, and he answered: "No, thank heaven, only a little cash!"

On his release from the hospital, he had left the service, had been "honourably discharged" with a medal for bravery, and had stayed on for an indefinite time in Europe, which he found "wonderful" and where he reveled in early dates. The French cathedrals, the Italian campaniles, *palazzi*, and galleries, the Swiss villages, a place like Stein am Rhein—all that was "most delightful indeed." And the wine everywhere, the *bistros* in France, the *trattorie* in Italy, the cosy *Wirtshäuser* in Switzerland and Germany, "at the sign of the Ox," "of the Moor," "of the Star" —where was there anything like that in America?

There was no wine there—just "drinks," whisky and rum, and no cool pints of Elsässer or Tiroler or Johannisberger at an oak table in a historical taproom or a honeysuckle arbour. Good heavens! People in America simply didn't know how to live.

Germany! That was the country he loved, though he really had explored it very little and in fact knew only the places on the Bodensee, and of course—but that he knew really well —the Rhineland. The Rhineland, with its charming, gay people, so amiable, especially when they were a bit "high"; with its venerable cities, full of atmosphere, Trier, Aachen, Coblenz, "Holy" Cologne—just try calling an American city "holy"—"Holy Kansas City," ha-ha! The golden treasure, guarded by the nixies of the Missouri River—ha-ha-ha—"Pardon me!" Of Düsseldorf and its long history from Merovingian days, he knew more than Rosalie and her children put together, and he spoke of Pepin the Short, of Barbarossa, who built the Imperial Palace at Rindhusen, and of the Salian Church at Kaiserswerth, where Henry IV was crowned King as a child, of Albert of Berg and John William of the Palatinate, and of many other things and people, like a professor.

Rosalie said that he could teach history too, just as well as English. There was too little demand, he replied. Oh, not at all, she protested. She herself, for instance, whom he had made keenly aware of how little she knew, would begin taking lessons from him at once. He would be "a little shy" about it, he confessed; in answer she expressed something that she had feelingly observed: It was strange and to a certain degree painful that in life shyness was the rule between youth and age. Youth was reserved in the presence of age because it expected no understanding of its green time of life from age's dignity, and age feared youth because, though admiring it whole-heartedly, simply as youth, age considered it due to its dignity to conceal its admiration under mockery and assumed condescension.

Ken laughed, pleased and approving. Eduard remarked that Mama really talked like a book, and Anna looked searchingly at her mother. She was decidedly vivacious in Mr. Keaton's presence, unfortunately even a little affected at times; she invited him frequently, and looked at him, even when he said "Pardon me" behind his hand, with an expression of motherly compassion which to Anna—who, despite the young man's enthusiasm for Europe, his passion for dates like 700, and his knowledge of all the time-honoured pothouses in Düsseldorf, found him totally uninteresting—appeared somewhat questionable in point of motherliness and made her not a little uncomfortable. Too often, when Mr. Keaton was to be present, her mother asked, with nervous apprehension, if her nose was flushed. It was, though Anna soothingly denied it. And if it wasn't before he arrived, it flushed with unwonted violence when she was in the young man's company. But then her mother seemed to have forgotten all about it.

ॐ

Anna saw rightly: Rosalie had begun to lose her heart to her son's young tutor, without offering any resistance to the rapid budding of her feeling, perhaps without being really aware of it, and in any case without making any particular

effort to keep it a secret. Symptoms that in another woman could not have escaped her feminine observation (a cooing and exaggeratedly
delighted laughter at Ken's chatter, a soulful
look followed by a curtaining of the brightened
eyes), she seemed to consider imperceptible in
herself—if she was not boasting of her feeling,
was not too proud of it to conceal it.

The situation became perfectly clear to the
suffering Anna one very summery, warm Sep-
tember evening, when Ken had stayed for dinner
and Eduard, after the soup, had asked permission,
on account of the heat, to take off his jacket.
The young men, was the answer, must feel no
constraint; and so Ken followed his pupil's example. He was not in the least concerned that,
whereas Eduard was wearing a colored shirt
with long sleeves, he had merely put on his jacket
over his sleeveless white jersey and hence now
displayed his bare arms—very handsome, round,
strong, white young arms, which made it perfectly comprehensible that he had been as good
at athletics in college as at history. The agitation
which the sight of them caused in the lady of the

house, he was certainly far from noticing, nor did Eduard have any eyes for it. But Anna observed it with pain and pity. Rosalie, talking and laughing feverishly, looked alternately as if she had been drenched with blood and frighteningly pale, and after every escape her fleeing eyes returned, under an irresistible attraction, to the young man's arms and then, for rapt seconds, lingered on them with an expression of deep and sensual sadness.

Anna, bitterly resentful of Ken's primitive guilelessness, which, however, she did not entirely trust, drew attention, as soon as she found even a shred of an excuse, to the evening coolness, which was just beginning to penetrate through the open French door, and suggested, with a warning against catching cold, that the jackets be put on again. But Frau von Tümmler terminated her evening almost immediately after dinner. Pretending a headache, she took a hurried leave of her guest and retired to her bedroom. There she lay stretched on her couch, with her face hidden in her hands and buried in the pillow, and, overwhelmed with shame, terror, and bliss, confessed her passion to herself.

"Good God, I love him, yes, love him, as I have never loved, is it possible? Here I am, retired from active service, translated by Nature to the calm, dignified estate of matronhood. Is it not grotesque that I should still give myself up to lust, as I do in my frightened, blissful thoughts at the sight of him, at the sight of his godlike arms, by which I insanely long to be embraced, at the sight of his magnificent chest, which, in wretchedness and rapture, I saw outlined under his jersey? Am I a shameless old woman? No, not shameless, for I am ashamed in his presence, in the presence of his youth, and I do not know how I ought to meet him and look him in the eyes, the ingenuous, friendly boy's eyes, which expect no burning emotion from me. But it is I who have been struck by the rod of life, he himself, all unknowing, has slashed me and peppered me with it, he has given me my Smack Easter! Why did he have to tell us of it, in his youthful enthusiasm for old folk customs? Now the thought of the awakening stroke of his rod leaves my inmost being drenched, inundated with shameful sweetness. I desire him—have I ever desired before? Tümmler desired me, when I was young, and I consented, acquiesced in his wooing, took him in marriage in his commanding manhood, and we gave ourselves up to lust when he desired. This time it is I who desire, of my own will and motion, and I have cast my eyes on him as a man casts his eyes on the young woman of his choice—this is what the years do, it is my age that does it and his youth. Youth is feminine, and age's relationship to it is masculine, but age is not happy and confident in its desire, it is full of shame and fear before youth and before all Nature, because of its unfitness. Oh, there is much sorrow in prospect for me, for how can I hope that he will be pleased by my desire, and, if pleased, that he will consent to my wooing, as I did to Tümmler's. He is no girl, with his firm arms, not he—far from it, he is a young man, who wants to desire for himself and who, they say, is very successful in that way with women. He has as many women as he wants, right here in town.

My soul writhes and screams with jealousy at the thought. He gives lessons in English conversation to Louise Pfingsten in Pempelforter Strasse and to Amélie Lützenkirchen, whose husband, the pottery-manufacturer, is fat, short-winded, and lazy. Louise is too tall and has a bad hairline, but she is only just thirty-eight and knows how to give melting looks. Amélie is only a little older, and pretty, unfortunately she is pretty, and that fat husband of hers gives her every liberty. Is it possible that they lie in his arms, or at least one of them does, probably Amélie, but it might be that stick of a Louise at the same time—in those arms for whose embrace I long with a fervour that their stupid souls could never muster? That they enjoy his hot breath, his lips, his hands that caress their bodies? My teeth, still so good, and which have needed so little attention—my teeth gnash, I gnash them, when I think of it. My figure too is better than theirs, worthier than theirs to be caressed by his hands, and what tenderness I should offer him, what inexpressible devotion! But they are flowing springs, and I am dried up, not worth being jealous of any more. Jealously,

torturing, tearing, crushing jealousy! That garden party at the Rollwagens'—the machine-fac-
tory Rollwagen and his wife—where he was invited too—wasn't it there that with my own
eyes, which see everything, I saw him and
Amélie exchange a look and a smile that almost
certainly pointed to some secret between them?
Even then my heart contracted with choking
pain, but I did not understand it, I did not think
it was jealousy because I no longer supposed myself capable of jealousy. But I am, I understand
that now, and I do not try to deny it, no, I rejoice in my torments—there they are, in marvellous disaccord with the physical change in me.
The psychological only an emanation of the
physical, says Anna, and the body moulds the
soul after its own condition? Anna knows a lot,
Anna knows nothing. No, I will not say that she
knows nothing. She has suffered, loved senseless-
ly and suffered shamefully, and so she knows a
great deal. But that soul and body are translated
together to the mild, honourable estate of matronhood—there she is all wrong, for she does
not believe in miracles, does not know that Na-

ture can make the soul flower miraculously, when
it is late, even too late—flower in love, desire, and
jealousy, as I am experiencing in blissful torment.
Sarah, the old grey crone, heard from behind the
tent door what was still appointed for her, and
she laughed. And God was angry with her and
said: Wherefore did Sarah laugh? I—I will not
have laughed. I will believe in the miracle of my
soul and my senses, I will revere the miracle Nature has wrought in me, this agonizing shy spring
in my soul, and I will be shamefaced only before
the blessing of this late visitation. . . ."

Thus Rosalie, communing with herself, on that
evening. After a night of violent restlessness and
a few hours of deep morning sleep, her first
thought on waking was of the passion that had
smitten her, blessed her, and to deny which, to
reject it on moral grounds, simply did not enter
her head. The poor woman was enraptured with
the survival in her soul of the ability to bloom in
sweet pain. She was not particularly pious, and
she left the Lord God out of the picture. Her
piety was for Nature, and it made her admire
and prize what Nature, as it were against herself,

had worked in her. Yes, it was contrary to natural seemliness, this flowering of her soul and senses; though it made her happy, it did not encourage her, it was something to be concealed, kept secret from all the world, even from her trusted daughter, but especially from him, her beloved, who suspected nothing and must suspect nothing—for how dared she boldly raise her eyes to his youth?

Thus into her relationship to Keaton there entered a certain submissiveness and humility which were completely absurd socially, yet which Rosalie, despite her pride in her feeling, was unable to banish from it, and which, on any clear-sighted observer—and so on Anna—produced a more painful effect than all the vivacity and excessive gaiety of her behaviour in the beginning. Finally even Eduard noticed it, and there were moments when brother and sister, bowed over their plates, bit their lips, while Ken, uncomprehendingly aware of the embarrassed silence, looked questioningly from one to another. Seeking counsel and enlightenment, Eduard took an opportunity to question his sister.

"What's happening to Mama?" he asked. "Doesn't she like Keaton any more?" And as Anna said nothing, the young man, making a wry face, added: "Or does she like him too much?"

"What are you thinking of?" was the reproving answer. "Such things are no concern of yours, at your age. Mind your manners, and do not permit yourself to make unsuitable observations!" But she went on: he might reverently remind himself that his mother, as all women eventually must, was having to go through a period of difficulties prejudicial to her health and well-being.

"Very new and instructive for me!" said the senior in school ironically; but the explanation was too general to suit him. Their mother was suffering from something more specific, and even she, his highly respected sister, was visibly suffering—to say nothing of his young and stupid self. But perhaps, young and stupid as he was, he could make himself useful by proposing the dismissal of his too attractive tutor. He had, he could tell his mother, got enough out of Keaton;

it was time for him to be "honourably discharged" again.

"Do so, dear Eduard," said Anna; and he did.

"Mama," he said, "I think we might stop my English lessons, and the constant expense I have put you to for them. Thanks to your generosity, I have laid a good foundation, with Mr. Keaton's help; and by doing some reading by myself I can see to it that it will not be lost. Anyway, no one ever really learns a foreign language at home, outside of the country where everybody speaks it and where one is entirely dependent on it. Once I am in England or America, after the start you have generously given me, the rest will come easily. As you know, my final examinations are approaching, and there is none in English. Instead I must see to it that I don't flunk the classical languages, and that requires concentration. So the time has come—don't you think?—to thank Keaton cordially for his trouble and in the most friendly way possible to dispense with his services."

"But Eduard," Frau von Tümmler answered at once, and indeed at first with a certain haste, "what you say surprises me, and I cannot say that I approve of it. Certainly, it shows great delicacy of feeling in you to wish to spare me further expenditure for this purpose. But the purpose is a good one, it is important for your future, as you now see it, and our situation is not such that we cannot meet the expenses of language lessons for you, quite as well as we were able to meet those of Anna's studies at the Academy. I do not understand why you want to stop halfway in your project to gain a mastery of the English language. It could be said, dear boy— please don't take it in bad part—that you would be making me an ill return for the willingness with which I met your proposal. Your final examinations—to be sure, they are a serious matter, and I understand that you will have to buckle down to your classical languages, which come hard to you. But your English lessons, a few times a week—you don't mean to tell me that they wouldn't be more of a recreation, a healthy distraction for you, than an additional strain. Besides—and now let me pass to the personal and human side of the matter—the relationship between Ken, as he is called, or rather Mr. Keaton, and our family has long since ceased to be such that we could say to him: 'You're no longer needed,' and simply give him his walking-papers. Simply announce: 'Sirrah, you may withdraw.' He has become a friend, almost a member of the family, and he would quite rightly be offended at such a dismissal. We should all feel his absence —Anna especially, I think, would be upset if he no longer came and enlivened our table with his intimate knowledge of the history of Düsseldorf, stopped telling us all about the quarrel over rights of succession between the duchies of Jülich and Cleves, and about Elector John William on his pedestal in the market place. You would miss him too, and so, in fact, should I. In short, Eduard, your proposal is well meant, but it is neither necessary nor, indeed, really possible. We had better leave things as they are."

"Whatever you think best, Mama," said Eduard, and reported his ill success to his sister, who answered:

"I expected as much, my boy. After all, Mama has described the situation quite correctly, and I saw much the same objections to your plan when you announced it to me. In any case, she is perfectly right in saying that Keaton is pleasant company and that we should all regret his absence. So just go on with him."

As she spoke, Eduard looked her in the face, which remained impassive; he shrugged his shoulders and left. Ken was waiting for him in his room, read a few pages of Emerson or Macaulay with him, then an American mystery story, which gave them something to talk about for the last half hour, and stayed for dinner, to which he had long since ceased to be expressly invited. His staying on after lessons had become a standing arrangement; and Rosalie, on the recurring days of her untoward and timorous, shame-clouded joy, consulted with Babette, the house-keeper, over the menu, ordered a choice repast, provided a full-bodied Pfälzer or Rüdesheimer, over which they would linger in the living-room for an hour after dinner, and to which she applied herself beyond her wont, so that she could look with better courage at the object of her unreasonable love. But often too the wine made her tired and desperate; and then whether she should stay and suffer in his sight or retire and weep over him in solitude became a battle which she fought with varying results.

October having brought the beginning of the social season, she also saw Keaton elsewhere than at her own house—at the Pfingstens' in Pempelforter Strasse, at the Lützenkirchens', at big receptions at Chief Engineer Rollwagen's. On these occasions she sought and shunned him, fled the group he had joined, waited in another, talking mechanically, for him to come and bestow some notice on her, knew at any moment where he was, listened for his voice amid the buzz of voices, and suffered horribly when she thought she saw signs of a secret understanding between him and Louise Pfingsten or Amélie Lützenkirchen. Although the young man had nothing in particular to offer except his fine physique, his complete naturalness and friendly simplicity, he was liked and sought out in this circle, contentedly profited by the German weakness for everything foreign, and knew very well that his pronunciation of German, the childish turns of phrase he used in speaking it, made a great hit. Then, too, people were glad to speak English with him. He could dress as he pleased. He had no evening clothes; social usages, however, had for many years been less strict, a dinner jacket was no longer absolutely obligatory in a box at the theater or at an evening party, and even on occasions where the majority of the gentlemen present wore evening dress, Keaton was welcome in ordinary street clothes, his loose, comfortable apparel, the belted brown trousers, brown shoes, and grey woollen jacket.

Thus unceremoniously he moved through drawing-rooms, made himself agreeable to the ladies to whom he gave English lessons, as well as to those by whom he would gladly have been prevailed upon to do the same—at table first cut a piece of his meat, then laid his knife diagonally across the rim of his plate, let his left arm hang, and, managing his fork with the right, ate what he had made ready. He adhered to this custom because he saw that the ladies on either side of him and the gentleman opposite observed it with such great interest.

He was always glad to chat with Rosalie, whether in company or tête-à-tête—not only because she was one of his sources of income but from a genuine attraction. For whereas her daughter's cool intelligence and intellectual pretensions inspired fear in him, the mother's true-hearted womanliness impressed him sympathetically, and, without correctly reading her feelings (it did not occur to him to do that), he allowed himself to bask in the warmth that radiated from her to him, took pleasure in it, and felt little concern over certain concomitant signs of tension, oppression, and confusion, which he interpreted as expressions of European nervousness and therefore held in high regard. In addition, for all her suffering, her appearance at this time acquired a conspicuous new bloom, a rejuvenescence, upon which she received many compliments. Her figure had always preserved its youthfulness, but what was so striking now was the light in her beautiful brown eyes—a light

which, if there was something feverish about it,
nevertheless added to her charm—was her heightened colouring, quick to return after occasional
moments of pallor, the mobility of feature that
characterized her face (it had become a little
fuller) in conversations that inclined to gaiety
and hence always enabled her to correct any
involuntary expression by a laugh. A good deal
of loud laughter was the rule at these convivial
gatherings, for all partook liberally of the wine
and punch, and what might have seemed eccen-
tric in Rosalie's manner was submerged in the
general atmosphere of relaxation, in which nothing caused much surprise. But how happy she
was when it happened that one of the women
said to her, in Ken's presence: "Darling, you are
astonishing! How ravishing you look this evening! You eclipse the girls of twenty. Do tell
me, what fountain of youth have you discovered?" And even more when her beloved cor-
roborated: "Right you are! Frau von Tümmler
is perfectly delightful tonight." She laughed, and
her deep blush could be attributed to her pleasure
in the flattery. She looked away from him, but

she thought of his arms, and again she felt the same prodigious sweetness drenching, inundating her inmost being—it had been a frequent sensation these days, and other women, she thought, when they found her young, when they found her charming, must surely be aware of it.

It was on one of these evenings, after the gathering had broken up, that she failed in her resolve to keep the secret of her heart, the illicit and painful but fascinating psychological miracle that had befallen her, wholly to herself and not to reveal it even to Anna's friendship. An irresistible need for communication forced her to break the promise she had made to herself and to confide in her brilliant daughter, not only because she yearned for understanding sympathy but also from a wish that what Nature was bringing to pass in her should be understood and honoured as the remarkable human phenomenon that it was.

A wet snow was falling; the two ladies had driven home through it in a taxicab about midnight. Rosalie was shivering. "Allow me, dear child," she said, "to sit up another half-hour with you in your cosy bedroom. I am freezing, but my head is on fire, and sleep, I fear, is out of the question for some time. If you would make tea for us, to end the evening, it wouldn't be a bad idea. That punch of the Rollwagens' is hard on one. Rollwagen mixes it himself, but he hasn't the happiest knack for it, pours a questionable orange cordial into the Moselle and then adds domestic champagne. Tomorrow we shall have terrible headaches again, a bad 'hangover.' Not you, that is. You are sensible and don't drink much. But I forget myself, chattering away, and don't notice that they keep filling my glass and think it is still the first. Yes, make tea for us, it's just the thing. Tea stimulates, but it soothes at the same time, and a cup of hot tea, taken at the right moment, wards off a cold. The rooms were far too hot at the Rollwagens'—at least, I thought so —and then the foul weather outdoors. Does it mean spring already? At noon today in the park I thought I really sniffed spring. But your silly mother always does that as soon as the shortest day has passed and the light increases again. A good idea, turning on the electric heater; there's not much heat left here at this hour. My dear child, you know how to make us comfortable and create just the right intimate atmosphere for a little tête-à-tête before we go to bed. You see, Anna, I have long wanted to have a talk with you, and—you are quite right—you have never denied me the opportunity. But there are things, child, to express which, to discuss which, requires a particularly intimate atmosphere, a favourable hour, which loosens one's tongue . . ."

"What sort of things, Mama? I haven't any cream to offer you. Will you take a little lemon?"

"Things of the heart, child, things of Nature, wonderful, mysterious, omnipotent Nature, who sometimes does such strange, contradictory, indeed incomprehensible things to us. You know it too. Recently, my dear Anna, I have found myself thinking a great deal about your old— forgive me for referring to it—your *affaire de cœur* with Brünner, about what you went through then, the suffering of which you complained to me in an hour not unlike this, and which, in bitter self-reproach, you even called a shame, because, that is, of the shameful conflict in which your reason, your judgment, was engaged with your heart, or, if you prefer, with your senses."

"You are quite right to change the word, Mama. 'Heart' is sentimental nonsense. It is inadmissible to say 'heart' for something that is entirely different. Our heart speaks truly only with the consent of our judgment and reason."

"You may well say so. For you have always been on the side of unity and insisted that Nature, simply of herself, creates harmony between soul and body. But that you were in a state of disharmony then—that is, between your wishes and your judgment—you cannot deny. You were very young at the time, and your desire had no reason to be ashamed in Nature's eyes, only in the eyes of your judgment, which called it debasing. It did not pass the test of your judgment, and that was your shame and your suffering. For you are proud, Anna, very proud; and that there might be a pride in feeling alone, a pride of feeling which denies that it has to pass the test of anything and be responsible to anything— judgment and reason and even Nature herself— that you will not admit, and in that we differ.

For to me the heart is supreme, and if Nature inspires feelings in it which no longer become it, and seems to create a contradiction between the heart and herself—certainly it is painful and shameful, but the shame is only for one's unworthiness and, at bottom, is sweet amazement, is reverence, before Nature and before the life that it pleases her to create in one whose life is done."

"My dear Mama," replied Anna, "let me first of all decline the honour that you accord to my pride and my reason. At the time, they would have miserably succumbed to what you poetically call my heart if a merciful fate had not intervened; and when I think where my heart would have led me, I cannot but thank God that I did not follow its desires. I am the last who would dare to cast a stone. However, we are not talking of me, but of you, and I will not decline the honour you accord me in wishing to confide in me. For that is what you wish to do, is it not? What you say indicates it, only you have spoken in such generalities that everything remains dark. Show me, please, how I am to refer them to you and how I am to understand them!"

"What should you say, Anna, if your mother, in her old age, were seized by an ardent feeling such as rightfully belongs only to potent youth, to maturity, and not to a withered womanhood?"

"Why the conditional, Mama? It is quite obvious that you are in the state you describe. You love?"

"How you say that, my sweet child! How freely and bravely and openly you speak the word which would not easily come to my lips, and which I have kept locked up in me so long, together with all the shameful joy and grief that it implies—have kept secret from everyone, even from you, so closely that you really had to be startled out of your dream, the dream of your belief in your mother's matronly dignity! Yes, I love, I love with ardour and desire and bliss and torment, as you once loved in your youth. My feeling can as little stand the test of reason as yours could, and if I am even proud of the spring with which Nature has made my soul flower, which she has miraculously bestowed upon me, I yet suffer, as you once suffered, and I have been irresistibly driven to tell you all."

"My dear, darling Mama! Then do tell me! When it is so hard to speak, questions help. Who is it?"

"It cannot but be a shattering surprise to you, my child. The young friend of the house. Your brother's tutor."

"Ken Keaton?"

"Yes."

"Ken Keaton. So that is it. You needn't fear, Mother, that I shall begin exclaiming 'Incomprehensible!'—though most people would. It is so easy and so stupid to call a feeling incomprehensible if one cannot imagine oneself having it. And yet—much as I want to avoid hurting you—forgive my anxious sympathy for asking a question. You speak of an emotion inappropriate to your years, complain of entertaining feelings of which you are no longer worthy. Have you ever asked yourself if he, this young man, is worthy of your feelings?"

"He—worthy? I hardly understand what you mean. I love, Anna. Of all the young men I have ever seen, Ken is the most magnificent."

"And that is why you love him. Shall we try

reversing the positions of cause and effect and perhaps get them in their proper places by doing so? May it not be that he only seems so magnificent to you because you are . . . because you love him?"

"Oh, my child, you separate what is inseparable. Here in my heart my love and his magnificence are one."

"But you are suffering, dearest, best Mama, and I should be so infinitely glad if I could help you. Could you not try, for a moment—just a moment of trying it might do you good—not to see him in the transfiguring light of your love, but by plain daylight, in his reality, as the nice, attractive—that I will grant you!—attractive lad he is, but who, such as he is, in and for himself, has so little to inspire passion and suffering on his account?"

"You mean well, Anna, I know. You would like to help me, I am sure of it. But it cannot be accomplished at his expense, by your doing him an injustice. And you do him injustice with your 'daylight,' which is such a false, misleading light. You say that he is nice, even attractive, and you mean by it that he is an average human being with nothing unusual about him. But I tell you he is an absolutely exceptional human being, with a life that touches one's heart. Think of his simple background—how, with iron strength of will, he worked his way through college, and excelled all his fellow students in history and athletics, and how he then hastened to his country's call and behaved so well as a soldier that he was finally 'honourably discharged' . . ."

"Excuse me, Mama, but that is the routine procedure for everyone who doesn't actually do something dishonourable."

"Everyone. You keep harping on his averageness, and, in doing so, by calling him, if not directly, then by implication, a simple-minded, ingenuous youngster, you mean to talk me out of him. But you forget that ingenuousness can be something noble and victorious, and that the background of his ingenuousness is the great democratic spirit of his immense country. . . ."

"He doesn't like his country in the least."

"And for that very reason he is a true son of it; and if he loves Europe for its historical per-

spectives and its old folk customs, that does him
honour too, and sets him apart from the majority.
And he gave his blood for his country. Every
soldier, you say, is 'honourably discharged.' But
is every soldier given a medal for bravery, a
Purple Heart, to show that the heroism with
which he flung himself on the enemy cost him
a wound, perhaps a serious one?"

"My dear Mama, in war, I think, one man
catches it and another doesn't, one falls and another escapes, without its having much to do with
whether he is brave or not. If somebody has a leg
blown off or a kidney shot to pieces, a medal is
a sop, a small compensation for his misfortune,
but in general it is no indication of any particular
bravery."

"In any case, he sacrificed one of his kidneys
on the altar of his fatherland!"

"Yes, he had that misfortune. And, thank
heaven, one can at a pinch make out with only
one kidney. But only at a pinch, and it *is* a lack,
a defect, the thought of it does rather detract
from the magnificence of his youth, and in the
common light of day, by which he ought to be

seen, does show him up, despite his good—or let us say normal—appearance, as not really complete, as disabled, as a man no longer perfectly whole."

"Good God—Ken no longer complete, Ken not a whole man! My poor child, he is complete to the point of magnificence and can laugh at the lack of a kidney—not only in his own opinion, but in everyone's—that is, in the opinion of all the women who are after him, and in whose company he seems to find his pleasure! My dear, good, clever Anna, don't you know why, above all other reasons, I have confided in you, why I began this conversation? Because I wished to ask you—and I want your honest opinion—if, from your observation, you believe that he is having an affair with Louise Pfingsten, or with Amélie Lützenkirchen, or perhaps with both of them—for which, I assure you, he is quite complete enough! That is what keeps me suspended in the most agonizing doubt, and I hope very much that I shall get the truth from you, for you can look at things more calmly, by daylight, so to speak. . . ."

"Poor, darling Mama, how you torture your-self, how you suffer! It makes me so unhappy. But, to answer you: I don't think so—of course, I know very little about his life and have not felt called upon to investigate it—but I don't think so, and I have never heard anyone say that he has the sort of relationship you suspect, either with Frau Pfingsten or Frau Lützenkirchen. So please be reassured, I beg of you!"

"God grant, dear child, that you are not sim-ply saying it to comfort me and pour balm on my wound, out of pity! But pity, don't you see, even though perhaps I am seeking it from you, is not in place at all, for I am happy in my tor-ment and shame and filled with pride in the flow-ering spring of pain in my soul—remember that, child, even if I seem to be begging for pity!"

"I don't feel that you are begging. But in such a case the happiness and pride are so closely al-lied with the suffering that, indeed, they are identical with it, and even if you looked for no pity, it would be your due from those who love you and who wish for you that you would take pity on yourself and try to free yourself from this

absurd enchantment. . . . Forgive my words;
they are the wrong ones, of course, but I cannot
be concerned over words. It is you, darling, for
whom I am concerned and not only since today,
not only since your confession, for which I am
grateful to you. You have kept your secret
locked within you with great self-control; but
that there has been some secret, that, for months
now, you have been in some peculiar and crucial
situation, could not escape those who love you,
and they have seen it with mixed feelings."

"To whom do you refer by your 'they'?"

"I am speaking of myself. You have changed
strikingly in these last weeks, Mama—I mean, not
changed, I'm not putting it right, you are still the
same, and if I say 'changed,' I mean that a sort
of rejuvenescence has come over you—but that
too isn't the right word, for naturally it can't be
a matter of any actual, demonstrable rejuvenescence in your charming person. But to my eyes,
at moments, and in a certain phantasmagoric
fashion, it has been as if suddenly, out of your
dear matronly self, stepped the Mama of twenty
years ago, as I knew her when I was a girl—and

even that was not all, I suddenly thought I saw you as I had never seen you, as you must have looked, that is, when you were a girl yourself. And this hallucination—if it was a mere hallucination, but there was something real about it too—should have delighted me, should have made my heart leap with pleasure, should it not? But it didn't, it only made my heart heavy, and at those very moments when you grew young before my eyes, I pitied you terribly. For at the same time I saw that you were suffering, and that the phantasmagoria to which I refer not only had to do with your suffering but was actually the expression of it, its manifestation, a 'flowering spring of pain,' as you just expressed it. Dear Mama, how did you happen to use such an expression? It is not natural to you. You are a simple being, worthy of all love; you have sound, clear eyes, you let them look into Nature and the world, not into books—you have never read much. Never before have you used expressions such as poets create, such lugubrious, sickly expressions, and if you do it now, it has a tinge of—"

"Of what, Anna? If poets use such expressions

it is because they *need* them, because emotion and experience force them out of them, and so it is, surely, with me, though you think them unbecoming in me. You are wrong. They are becoming to whoever needs them, and he has no fear of them, because they are forced out of him. But your hallucination, or phantasmagoria—whatever it was that you thought you saw in me—I can and will explain to you. It was the work of *his* youth. It was my soul's struggle to match his youth, so that it need not perish before him in shame and disgrace."

Anna wept. They put their arms around each other, and their tears mingled.

"That too," said the lame girl with an effort, "what you have just said, dear heart, that too is of a piece with the strange expression you used, and, like that, coming from your lips, it has a ring of destruction. This accursed seizure is destroying you, I see it with my eyes, I hear it in your speech. We must check it, put a stop to it, save you from it, at any cost. One forgets, Mama, what is out of one's sight. All that is needed is a decision, a saving decision. The young man must not come here any longer, we must dismiss him. That is not enough. You see him elsewhere when you go out. Very well, we must prevail upon him to leave the city. I will take it upon myself to persuade him. I will talk to him in a friendly way, point out to him that he is wasting his time and himself here, that he has long since exhausted Düsseldorf and should not hang around here forever, that Düsseldorf is not Germany, of which he must see more, get to know it better, that Munich, Hamburg, Berlin are there for him to sample, that he must not let himself be tied down, must live in one place for a time, then in another, until, as is his natural duty, he returns to his own country and takes up a regular profession, instead of playing the invalid language-teacher here in Europe. I'll soon impress it upon him. And if he declines and insists on sticking to Düsseldorf, where, after all, he has connections, we will go away ourselves. We will give up our house here and move to Cologne or Frankfurt or to some lovely place in the Taunus, and you will leave here behind you what has been torturing you and trying to destroy you, and with the help of 'out of sight,' you will forget. Out of sight—it is all that is needed, it is an infallible remedy, for there is no such thing as not being able to forget. You may say it is a disgrace to forget, but people do forget, depend upon it. And in the Taunus you will enjoy your beloved Nature and you will be our old darling Mama again."

Thus Anna, with great earnestness, but how unavailingly!

"Stop, stop, Anna, no more of this, I cannot listen to what you are saying! You weep with me, and your concern is affectionate indeed, but what you say, your proposals, are impossible and shocking to me. Drive him away? Leave here ourselves? How far your solicitude has led you astray! You speak of Nature, but you strike her in the face with your demands, you want me to strike her in the face, by stifling the spring of pain with which she has miraculously blest my soul! What a sin that would be, what ingratitude, what disloyalty to her, to Nature, and what a denial of my faith in her beneficent omnipotence! You remember how Sarah sinned? She laughed to herself behind the door and said:

'After I am waxed old shall I have pleasure, my
lord being old also?' But the Lord God was
angry and said: 'Wherefore did Sarah laugh?' In
my opinion, she laughed less on account of her
own withered old age than because her lord,
Abraham, was likewise so old and stricken in
years, already ninety-nine. And what woman
could not but laugh at the thought of indulging
in lust with a ninety-nine-year-old man, for all
that a man's love life is less strictly limited than
a woman's. But my lord is young, is youth itself,
and how much more easily and temptingly must
the thought come to me— Oh, Anna, my loyal
child, I indulge in lust, shameful and grievous
lust, in my blood, in my wishes, and I cannot give
it up, cannot flee to the Taunus, and if you persuade Ken to go—I believe I should hate you to
my dying day!"

Great was the sorrow with which Anna listened to these unrestrained, frenzied words.

"Dearest Mama," said she in a strained voice,
"you are greatly excited. What you need now is
rest and sleep. Take twenty drops of valerian in
water, or even twenty-five. It is a harmless rem-

edy and often very helpful. And rest assured
that, for my part, I will undertake nothing that is
opposed to your feeling. May this assurance help
to bring you the peace of mind which, above all
things, I desire for you! If I spoke slightingly of
Keaton, whom I respect as the object of your affection, though I cannot but curse him as the
cause of your suffering, you will understand that
I was only trying to see if it would not restore
your peace of mind. I am infinitely grateful for
your confidence, and I hope, indeed I am sure,
that by talking to me you have somewhat light-
ened your heart. Perhaps this conversation was
the prerequisite for your recovery—I mean, for
your restored peace of mind. Your sweet, happy
heart, so dear to us all, will find itself again. It
loves in pain. Do you not think that—let us say,
in time—it could learn to love without pain and
in accordance with reason? Love, don't you
see?—" (Anna said this as she solicitously led her
mother to her bedroom, so that she could herself
drop the valerian into her glass) "love—how
many things it is, what a variety of feelings are
included in the word, and yet how strangely it is

always love! A mother's love for her son, for instance—I know that Eduard is not particularly close to you—but that love can be very heartfelt, very passionate, it can be subtly yet clearly distinguished from her love for a child of her own sex, and yet not for an instant pass the bounds of mother love. How would it be if you were to take advantage of the fact that Ken could be your son, to make the tenderness you feel for him maternal, let it find a permanent place, to your own benefit, as mother love?"

Rosalie smiled through her tears.

"And thus establish the proper understanding between body and soul, I take it?" she jested sadly. "My dear child, the demands that I make on your intelligence! How I exhaust it and misuse it! It is wrong of me, for I trouble you to no purpose. Mother love—it is something like the Taunus all over again. . . . Perhaps I'm not expressing myself quite clearly now? I *am* dead tired, you are right about that. Thank you, darling, for your patience, your sympathy! Thank you too for respecting Ken for the sake of what you call my affection. And don't hate him at the same time, as I should have to hate you if you drove him away! He is Nature's means of working her miracle in my soul."

ॐ

Anna left her. A week passed, during which Ken Keaton twice dined at the Tümmlers'. The first time, an elderly couple from Duisburg were present, relatives of Rosalie's; the woman was a cousin of hers. Anna, who well knew that certain relationships and emotional tensions inevitably emanate an aura that is obvious particularly to those who are in no way involved, observed the guests keenly. Once or twice she saw Rosalie's cousin look wonderingly first at Keaton, then at the hostess; once she even detected a smile under the husband's moustache. That evening she also observed a difference in Ken's behaviour toward her mother, a quizzical change and readjustment in his reactions, observed too that he would not let it pass when, laboriously enough, she pretended not to be taking any particular notice of him, but forced her to direct her attention to him. On the second occasion no one else was present. Frau von Tümmler indulged in a scurrilous performance, directed at her daughter and inspired by her recent conversation with her, in which she mocked at certain of Anna's counsels and at the same time turned the travesty to her own advantage. It had come out that Ken had been very much on the town the previous night—with a few of his cronies, an art-school student and two sons of manufacturers, he had gone on a pub-crawl that had lasted until morning, and, as might have been expected, had arrived at the Tümmlers' with a "first-class hangover," as Eduard, who was the one to let out the story, expressed it. At the end of the evening, when the good-nights were being said, Rosalie gave her daughter a look that was at once excited and crafty—indeed, kept her eyes fixed on her for a moment as she held the young man by the lobe of his ear and said:

"And you, son, take a serious word of reproof from Mama Rosalie and understand hereafter that her house is open only to people of decent behaviour and not to night-owls and disabled beer-swillers who are hardly up to speaking German or even to keeping their eyes open! Did you hear me, you good-for-nothing? Mend your ways! If bad boys tempt you, don't listen to them, and from now on stop playing so fast and loose with your health! Will you mend your ways, will you?" As she spoke, she kept tugging at his ear, and Ken yielded to the slight pull in an exaggerated way, pretended that the punishment was extraordinarily painful, and writhed under her hand with a most pitiable grimace, which showed his fine white teeth. His face was near to hers, and speaking directly into it, in all its nearness, she went on:

"Because if you do it again and don't mend your ways, you naughty boy, I'll banish you from the city—do you know that? I'll send you to some quiet place in the Taunus where, though Nature is very beautiful, there are no temptations and you can teach the farmers' children English. This time, go and sleep it off, you scamp!" And she let go of his ear, took leave of the nearness of his face, gave Anna one more pale, crafty look, and left.

A week later something extraordinary happened, which astonished, touched, and perplexed

Anna von Tümmler in the highest degree—perplexed her because, though she rejoiced in it for her mother's sake, she did not know whether to regard it as fortunate or unfortunate. About ten o'clock in the morning the chambermaid brought a message asking her to see the mistress in her bedroom. Since the little family breakfasted separately—Eduard first, then Anna, the lady of the house last—she had not yet seen her mother that day. Rosalie was lying on the chaise longue in her bedroom, covered with a light cashmere blanket, a little pale, but with her nose flushed. With a smile of rather studied languor, she nodded to her daughter as she came stumping in, but said nothing, so that Anna was forced to ask:

"What is it, Mama? You aren't ill, are you?"

"Oh no, my child, don't be alarmed, I'm not ill at all. I was very much tempted, instead of sending for you, to go to you myself and greet you. But I am a little in need of coddling, rest seems to be indicated, as it sometimes is for us women."

"Mama! What do you mean?"

Then Rosalie sat up, flung her arms around her

daughter's neck, drew her down beside her onto the edge of the chaise longue, and, cheek to cheek with her, whispered in her ear, quickly, blissfully, all in a breath:

"Victory, Anna, victory, it has come back to me, come back to me after such a long interruption, absolutely naturally and just as it should be for a mature, vigorous woman! Dear child, what a miracle! What a miracle great, beneficent Nature has wrought in me, how she has blessed my faith! For I believed, Anna, and did not laugh, and so now kind Nature rewards me and takes back what she seemed to have done to my body, she proves that it was a mistake and re-establishes harmony between soul and body, but not in the way that you wished it to happen. Not with the soul obediently letting the body act upon it and translate it to the dignified estate of matronhood, but the other way around, the other way around, dear child, with the soul proving herself mistress over the body. Congratulate me, darling, there is reason for it! I am a woman again, a whole human being again, a functioning female, I can feel worthy of the youthful manhood that has bewitched me, and no longer need lower my eyes before it with a feeling of impotence. The rod of life with which it struck me has reached not my soul alone but my body too and has made it a flowing fountain again. Kiss me, my darling child, call me blessed, as blessed I am, and, with me, praise the miraculous power of great, beneficent Nature!"

She sank back, closed her eyes, and smiled contentedly, her nose very red.

"Dear, sweet Mama," said Anna, willing enough to rejoice with her, yet sick at heart, "this is truly a great, a moving event, it testifies to the richness of your nature, which was already evident in the freshness of your feeling and now gives that feeling such power over your bodily functions. As you see, I am entirely of your opinion—that what has happened to you physically is psychological in origin, is the product of your youthfully strong feeling. Whatever I may at times have said about such things, you must not think me such a Philistine that I deny the psychological any power over the physical and hold that the latter has the last word in the relationship between them. Each is dependent upon the other—that much even I know about Nature and its unity. However much the soul may be subject to the body's circumstances—what the soul, for its part, can do to the body often verges on the miraculous, and your case is one of the most splendid examples of it. Yet, permit me to say that this beautiful, animating event, of which you are so proud—and rightly, you may certainly be proud of it—on me, constituted as I am, it does not make the same sort of impression that it makes on you. In my opinion, it does not change things much, my best of mothers, and it does not appreciably increase my admiration for your nature—or for Nature in general. Clubfooted, aging spinster that I am, I have every reason not to attach much importance to the physical. Your freshness of feeling, precisely in contrast to your physical age, seemed to me splendid enough, enough of a triumph—it almost seemed to me a purer victory of the soul than what has happened now, than this transformation of the indestructible youth of your heart into an organic phenomenon."

"Say no more, my poor child! What you call my freshness of feeling, and now insist that you enjoyed, you represented to me, more or less bluntly, as sheer folly, through which I was making myself ridiculous, and you advised me to re-retreat into a motherly dowagerhood, to make my feeling maternal. Well, it would have been a little too early for that, don't you think so now, my pet? Nature has made her voice heard against it. She has made my feeling her concern and has unmistakably shown me that it need not be ashamed before her nor before the blooming young manhood which is its object. And do you really mean to say that does not change things much?"

"What I mean, my dear, wonderful Mama, is certainly not that I did not respect Nature's voice. Nor, above all things, do I wish to spoil your joy in her decree. You cannot think that of me. When I said that what had happened did not change things much, I was referring to outward realities, to the practical aspects of the situation, so to speak. When I advised you—when I fondly wished that you might conquer yourself, that it might not even be hard for you to confine your feeling for the young man—forgive me for speaking of him so coolly—for our friend Keaton, rather, to maternal love, my hope was based on the fact that he could be your son. That fact, you will agree, has not changed, and it cannot but determine the relationship between you on either side, on your side and on his too."

"And on his too. You speak of two sides, but you mean only his. You do not believe that he could love me except, at best, as a son?"

"I will not say that, dearest and best Mama."

"And how could you say it, Anna, my true-hearted child! Remember, you have no right to, you have not the necessary authority to judge in matters of love. You have little perception in that realm, because you gave up early, dear heart, and turned your eyes away from such things. Intellect offered you a substitute for Nature— good for you, that is all very fine! But how can you undertake to judge and to condemn me to hopelessness? You have no power of observation and do not see what I see, do not perceive the signs which indicate to me that his feeling is

ready to respond to mine. Do you mean to say
that at such moments he is only trifling with me?
Would you rather consider him insolent and
heartless than to grant me the hope that his feeling may correspond to mine? What would be so
extraordinary in that? For all your aloofness
from love, you cannot be unaware that a young
man very often prefers a mature woman to an
inexperienced girl, to a silly little goose. Naturally, a nostalgia for his mother may enter in—
as, on the other hand, maternal feelings may play
a part in an elder woman's passion for a young
man. But why say this to you? I have a distinct
impression that you recently said something very
like it to me."

"Really? In any case, you are right, Mama.
I agree with you completely in what you say."

"Then you must not call me past hope, especially today, when Nature has recognized my
feeling. You must not, despite my grey hair, at
which, so it seems to me, you are looking. Yes,
unfortunately I am quite grey. It was a mistake
that I didn't begin dyeing my hair long ago. I
can't suddenly start now, though Nature has to

a certain extent authorized me to. But I can do something for my face, not only by massage, but also by using a little rouge. I don't suppose you children would be shocked?"

"Of course not, Mama! Eduard will never notice, if you go about it a little discreetly. And I . . . though I think that artificiality will not go too well with your deep feeling for Nature, why, it is certainly no sin against Nature to help her out a little in such an accepted fashion."

"So you agree with me? After all, the thing is to prevent a fondness for being mothered from playing too large a part, from predominating, in Ken's feeling. That would be contrary to my hopes. Yes, dear, loyal child, this heart—I know that you do not like talking and hearing about the 'heart'—but my heart is swollen with pride and joy, with the thought of how very differently I shall now meet his youth, with what a different self-confidence. Your mother's heart is swollen with happiness and life!"

"How beautiful, dearest Mama! And how charming of you to let me share in your great happiness! I share it, share it from my heart, you cannot doubt it, even if I say that a certain concern intrudes even as I rejoice with you—that is very like me, isn't it?—certain scruples—*practical* scruples, to use the word which, for want of a better, I used before. You speak of your hope, and of all that justifies you in entertaining it— in my opinion, what justifies it above all is simply your own lovable self. But you fail to define your hope more precisely, to tell me what its goal is, what expression it expects to find in the reality of life. Is it your intention to marry again? To make Ken Keaton our stepfather? To stand before the altar with him? It may be cowardly of me, but as the difference in your ages is equivalent to that between a mother and her son, I am a little afraid of the astonishment which such a step would arouse."

Frau von Tümmler stared at her daughter.

"No," she answered, "the idea is new to me, and if it will calm your apprehensions, I can assure you that I do not entertain it. No, Anna, you silly thing, I have no intention of giving you and

Eduard a twenty-four-year-old stepfather. How odd of you to speak so stiffly and piously of 'standing before the altar'!"

Anna remained silent; her eyelids lowered a little, she gazed past her mother into space.

"Hope—" said her mother, "who can define it, as you want me to? Hope is hope—how can you expect that it will inquire into practical goals, as you put it? What Nature has granted me is so beautiful that I can only expect something beautiful from it, but I cannot tell you how I think that it will come, how it will be realized, and where it will lead. That is what hope is like. It simply doesn't think—least of all about 'standing before the altar.' "

Anna's lips were slightly twisted. Between them she spoke softly, as if involuntarily and despite herself:

"That would be a comparatively reasonable idea."

Frau von Tümmler stared in bewilderment at her crippled daughter—who did not look at her —and tried to read her expression.

"Anna!" she cried softly. "What are you thinking, what does this behaviour mean? Allow me to say that I simply don't recognize you! Which of us, I ask you, is the artist—I or you? I should never have thought that you could be so far behind your mother in broad-mindedness —and not only behind her, but behind the times and its freer manners! In your art you are so advanced and profess the very latest thing, so that a simple person like myself can scarcely follow you. But morally you seem to be living God knows when, in the old days, before the war. After all, we have the republic now, we have freedom, and ideas have changed very much, toward informality, toward laxity, it is apparent everywhere, even in the smallest things. For example, nowadays young men consider it good form to let their handkerchiefs, of which you used to see only a little corner protruding from the breast pocket, hang far out—why, they let them hang out like flags, half the handkerchief; it is clearly a sign, even a conscious declaration, of a republican relaxation of manners. Eduard lets his handkerchief hang out too, in the way that is the fashion, and I see it with a certain satisfaction."

"Your observation is very fine, Mama. But I think that, in Eduard's case, your handkerchief symbol is not to be taken too personally. You yourself often say that the young man—for such by this time he has really become—is a good deal like our father, the lieutenant-colonel. Perhaps it is not quite tactful of me to bring Papa into our conversation and our thoughts at the moment. And yet—"

"Anna, your father was an excellent officer and he fell on the field of honour, but he was a rake and a Don Juan to the very end, the most striking example of the elastic limits of a man's sexual life, and I constantly had to shut both eyes on his account. So I cannot consider it particularly tactless that you should refer to him."

"All the better, Mama—if I may say so. But Papa was a gentleman and an officer, and he lived, despite all that you call his rakishness, according to certain concepts of honour, which mean very little to me, but many of which Eduard, I believe, has inherited. He not only resembles his father outwardly, in figure and features. Under certain circumstances, he will involuntarily react in his father's fashion."

"Which means—under what circumstances?"

"Dear Mama, let me be perfectly frank, as we have always been with each other! It is certainly conceivable that a relationship such as you vaguely anticipate between Ken Keaton and yourself could remain completely concealed and unknown to society. However, what with your delightful impulsiveness and your charming inability to dissimulate and bury the secrets of your heart, I have my doubts as to how well it could be carried off. Let some young whipper-snapper make mocking allusions to our Eduard, give him to understand that it is known that his mother is —how do people put it?—leading a loose life, and he would strike him, he would box the fellow's ears, and who knows what dangerous kind of official nonsense might result from his chivalry?"

"For heaven's sake, Anna! What things you imagine! You are excruciating. I know you are doing it out of solicitude, but it is cruel, your solicitude, as cruel as small children condemning their mother. . . ."

Rosalie cried a little. Anna helped her to dry her tears, affectionately guiding the hand in which she held her handkerchief.

"Dearest, best Mama, forgive me! How reluctant I am to hurt you! But you—don't talk of children condemning! Do you think I would not look—no, not tolerantly, that sounds too supercilious—but reverently, and with the tenderest concern, on what you are determined to consider your happiness? And Eduard—I hardly know how I happened to speak of him—it was just because of his republican handkerchief. It is not a question of us, nor only of people in general. It is a question of you, Mama. Now, you said that you were broad-minded. But are you, really? We were speaking of Papa and of certain traditional concepts by which he lived, and which, as he saw them, were not infringed by the infidelities he upset you with. That you forgave him for them again and again was because, fundamentally, as you must realize, you were of the same opinion—you were, in other words, conscious that they had nothing to do with real debauchery. He was not born for that, he was no libertine at heart. No more are you. I, at most, as an artist, have deviated from type in that respect, but then again, in another way, I am unfitted to make use of my emancipation, of my being morally *déclassée*."

"My poor child," Frau von Tümmler interrupted her, "don't speak of yourself so gloomily!"

"As if I were speaking of myself at all!" answered Anna. "I am speaking of you, of you, it is for you that I am so deeply concerned. Because, for you, it would really be debauchery to do what, for Papa, the man about town, was simply dissipation, doing violence neither to himself nor to the judgment of society. Harmony between body and soul is certainly a good and necessary thing, and you are proud and happy because Nature, your beloved Nature, has granted it to you in a way that is almost miraculous. But harmony between one's life and one's innate moral convictions is, in the end, even more necessary, and where it is disrupted the only result

can be emotional disruption, and that means un-
happiness. Don't you feel that this is true? That
you would be living in opposition to yourself if
you made a reality out of what you now dream?
Fundamentally, you are just as much bound as
Papa was to certain concepts, and the destruction
of that allegiance would be no less than the destruction of your own self. . . . I say it as I feel
it—with anxiety. Why does that word come to
my lips again—'destruction'? I know that I have
used it once before, in anguish, and I have had
the sensation more than once. Why must I keep
feeling as if this whole visitation, whose happy
victim you are, had something to do with destruction? I will confess something to you. Recently, just a few weeks ago, after our talk when
we drank tea late that night in my room and you
were so excited, I was tempted to go to Dr. Oberloskamp, who took care of Eduard when he had
jaundice, and of me once, when I had laryngitis
and couldn't swallow—you never need a doctor;
I was tempted, I say, to talk to him about you
and about what you had confided to me, simply

for the sake of setting my mind at rest on your account. But I rejected the idea, I rejected it almost at once, out of pride, Mama, out of pride in you and for you, and because it seemed to me degrading to turn your experience over to a medical man who, with the help of God, is competent for jaundice and laryngitis, but not for deep human ills. In my opinion, there are sicknesses that are too good for the doctor."

"I am grateful to you for both, my dear child," said Rosalie, "for the concern which impelled you to talk with Oberloskamp about me, and for your having repressed the impulse. But then what can induce you to make the slightest connection between what you call my visitation—this Easter of my womanhood, what the soul has done to my body—and the concept of sickness? Is happiness—sickness? Certainly, it is not light-mindedness either, it is living, living in joy and sorrow, and to live is to hope—the hope for which I can give no explanation to your reason."

"I do not ask for any explanation from you, dearest Mama."

"Then go now, child. Let me rest. As you know, a little quiet seclusion is indicated for us women on such crowning days."

ॐ

Anna kissed her mother and stumped out of the bedroom. Once separated, the two women reflected on the conversation they had just held. Anna had neither said, nor been able to say, all that was on her mind. How long, she wondered, would what her mother called "the Easter of her womanhood," this touching revivification, endure in her? And Ken, if, as was perfectly plausible, he succumbed to her—how long would *that* last? How constantly her mother, in her late love, would be cast into trepidation by every younger woman, would have to tremble, from the very first day, for his faithfulness, even his respect! At least it was to the good that she did not conceive of happiness simply as pleasure and joy but as life with its suffering. For Anna uneasily foresaw much suffering in what her mother dreamed.

For her part, Frau Rosalie was more deeply impressed by her daughter's remonstrances than she had allowed to appear. It was not so much the thought that, under certain circumstances, Eduard might have to risk his young life for her honour—the romantic idea, though she had wept over it, really made her heart beat with pride. But Anna's doubts of her "broad-mindedness," what she had said about debauchery and the necessary harmony between one's life and one's moral convictions, preoccupied the good soul all through her day of rest and she could not but admit that her daughter's doubts were justified, that her views contained a good part of truth. Neither, to be sure, could she suppress her most heartfelt joy at the thought of meeting her young beloved again under such new circumstances. But what her shrewd daughter had said about "living in contradiction to herself," she remembered and pondered over, and she strove in her soul to associate the idea of renunciation with the idea of happiness. Yes, could not renunciation itself be happiness, if it were not a miserable necessity but were practiced in freedom and in conscious equality? Rosalie reached the conclusion that it could be.

Ken presented himself at the Tümmlers' three

days after Rosalie's great physiological reas-
surance, read and spoke English with Eduard,
and stayed for dinner. Her happiness at the sight
of his pleasant, boyish face, his fine teeth, his
broad shoulders and narrow hips, shone from her
sweet eyes, and their sparkling animation justified, one might say, the touch of artificial red
which heightened her cheeks and without which,
indeed, the pallor of her face would have been
in contradiction to that joyous fire. This time,
and thereafter every time Ken came, she had a
way, each week, of taking his hand when she
greeted him and drawing his body close to hers,
at the same time looking earnestly, luminously,
and significantly into his eyes, so that Anna had
the impression that she very much wished, and
indeed was going, to tell the young man of the
experience her nature had undergone. Absurd
apprehension! Of course nothing of the sort oc-
curred, and all through the rest of the evening
the attitude of the lady of the house toward her
young guest was a serene and settled kindliness
from which both the affected motherliness with
which she had once teased her daughter, as well

as any bashfulness and nervousness, any painful humility, were gratifyingly absent.

Keaton, who to his satisfaction had long been aware that, even such as he was, he had made a conquest of this grey-haired but charming European woman, hardly knew what to make of the change in her behaviour. His respect for her had, quite understandably, diminished when he became aware of her weakness; the latter, on the other hand, had in turn attracted and excited his masculinity; his simple nature felt sympathetically drawn to hers, and he considered that such beautiful eyes, with their youthful, penetrating gaze, quite made up for fifty years and aging hands. The idea of entering into an affair with her, such as he had been carrying on for some time—not, as it happened, with Amélie Lützenkirchen or Louise Pfingsten, but with another woman of the same set, whom Rosalie had never thought of—was by no means new to him, and, as Anna observed, he had begun, at least now and again, to change his manner toward his pupil's mother, to speak to her in a tone that was provocatively flirtatious.

This, the good fellow soon found, no longer seemed quite to come off. Despite the handclasp by which, at the beginning of each meeting, she drew him close to her, so that their bodies almost touched, and despite her intimate, searching gaze into his eyes, his experiments in this direction encountered a friendly but firm dignity which put him in his place, forbade any establishment of what he wished to establish, and, instantly dispelling his pretensions, reduced his attitude to one of submission. The meaning of the repeated experience escaped him. "Is she in love with me or not?" he asked himself, and blamed her repulses and her reprobation on the presence of her children, the lame girl and the schoolboy. But his experience was no different when it happened that he was alone with her for a time in a drawing-room corner—and no different when he changed the character of his little advances, abandoning all quizzicalness and giving them a seriously tender, a pressing, almost passionate tone. Once, using the unrolled palatal "r" which so delighted everyone, he tried calling her "Rosalie" in a warm voice—which, simply as a form

of address, was, in his American view, not even
a particular liberty. But, though for an instant
she had blushed hotly, she had almost immediately risen and left him, and had given him neither
a word nor a look during the rest of that evening.

The winter, which had proved to be mild,
bringing hardly any cold weather and snow, but
all the more rain instead, also ended early that
year. Even in February there were warm, sunny
days redolent of spring. Tiny leaf buds ventured
out on branches here and there. Rosalie, who
had lovingly greeted the snowdrops in her garden, could rejoice far earlier than usual, almost
prematurely, in the daffodils—and, very soon
after, in the short-stemmed crocuses too, which
sprouted everywhere in the front gardens of
villas and in the Palace Garden, and before
which passers-by halted to point them out to one
another and to feast on their particoloured pro-
fusion.

"Isn't it remarkable," said Frau von Tümmler
to her daughter, "how much they resemble the
autumn colchicum? It's practically the same
flower! End and beginning—one could mistake

them for each other, they are so alike—one could think one was back in autumn in the presence of a crocus, and believe in spring when one saw the last flower of the year."

"Yes, a slight confusion," answered Anna. "Your old friend Mother Nature has a charming propensity for the equivocal and for mystification in general."

"You are always quick to speak against her, you naughty child, and where I succumb to wonder, you mock. Let well enough alone; you cannot laugh me out of my tender feeling for her, for my beloved Nature, least of all now, when she is just bringing in my season—I call it mine because the season in which we were born is peculiarly akin to us, and we to it. You are an Advent child, and you can truly say that you arrived under a good sign—almost under the dear sign of Christmas. You must feel a pleasant affinity between yourself and that season, which, even though cold, makes us think of joy and warmth. For really, in my experience, there is a sympathetic relation between ourselves and the season that produced us. Its return brings something that confirms and strengthens, that renews our lives, just as spring has always done for me—not because it is spring, or the prime of the year, as the poets call it, a season everyone loves, but because I personally belong to it, and I feel that it smiles at me quite personally."

"It does indeed, dearest Mama," answered the child of winter. "And rest assured that I shan't speak a single word against it!"

But it must be said that the buoyancy of life which Rosalie was accustomed—or believed she was accustomed—to receive from the approach and unfolding of "her" season was not, even as she spoke of it, manifesting itself quite as usual. It was almost as if the moral resolutions which her conversation with her daughter had inspired in her, and to which she so steadfastly adhered, went against her nature, as if, despite them, or indeed because of them, she were "living in contradiction to herself." This was precisely the impression that Anna received, and the limping girl reproached herself for having persuaded her mother to a continence which her own liberal view of life in no sense demanded but which had seemed requisite to her only for the dear woman's peace of mind. What was more, she suspected herself of unacknowledged evil motives. She asked herself if she, who had once grievously longed for sensual pleasure, but had never experienced it, had not secretly begrudged it to her mother and hence had exhorted her to chastity by all sorts of trumped-up arguments. No, she could not believe it of herself, and yet what she saw troubled and burdened her conscience.

She saw that Rosalie, setting out on one of the walks she so loved, quickly grew tired, and that it was she who, inventing some household task that must be done, insisted on turning home after only half an hour or even sooner. She rested a great deal, yet despite this limitation of her physical activity, she lost weight, and Anna noticed with concern the thinness of her forearms when she happened to see them exposed. People no longer asked her at what fountain of youth she had been drinking. There was an ominous, tired-looking blueness under her eyes, and the rouge which, in honour of the young man and of her recovery of full womanhood, she put on her cheeks created no very effective illusion against the yellowish pallor of her complexion. But as she dismissed any inquiries as to how she felt with a cheerful, "I feel quite well—why should you think otherwise?" Fräulein von Tümmler gave up the idea of asking Dr. Oberloskamp to investigate her mother's failing health. It was not only a feeling of guilt which led her to this decision; piety too played a part—the same piety that she had expressed when she said that there were sicknesses which were too good to be taken to a doctor.

ॐ

So Anna was all the more delighted by the enterprise and confidence in her strength which Rosalie exhibited in connection with a little plan that was agreed on between herself, her children, and Ken Keaton, who happened to be present, one evening as they lingered over their wine. A month had not yet passed since the morning Anna had been called to her mother's bedroom to hear the wonderful news. Rosalie was as charming and gay as in the old days that evening, and she could have been considered the prime

mover of the excursion on which they had agreed
—unless Ken Keaton was to be given the credit,
for it was his historical chatter that had led to
the idea. He had talked about various castles and
strongholds he had visited in the Duchy of Berg
—of the Castle on the Wupper, of Bensberg,
Ehreshoven, Gimhorn, Homburg, and Krot-
torf; and from these he went on to the Elector
Carl Theodore, who, in the eighteenth century,
had moved his court from Düsseldorf, first to
Schwetzingen and then to Munich—but that had
not prevented his Statthalter, a certain Count
Grottstein, from embarking on all sorts of important architectural and horticultural projects
here: it was under him that the Electoral Academy of Art was conceived, the Palace Garden
was first laid out, and Jägerhof Castle was built
—and, Eduard added, in the same year, so far as
he knew, Holterhof Castle too, a little to the
south of the city, near the village of the same
name. Of course, Holterhof too, Keaton confirmed, and then, to his own amazement, was
obliged to admit that he had never laid eyes on
that creation of the late Rococo nor even visited

its park, celebrated as it was, which extended all the way to the Rhine. Frau von Tümmler and Anna had, of course, taken the air there once or twice, but they had never got around to viewing the interior of the charmingly situated castle, nor had Eduard.

"Wat et nit all jibt!" said the lady of the house, using, in jocular disapproval, the local equivalent of "Will wonders never cease!" It was always an indication of good spirits when she dropped into dialect. "Fine Düsseldorfers you are," she added, "all four of you!" One had never been there at all, and the others had not seen the interior of the jewel of a castle which every tourist made it a point to be shown through! "Children," she cried, "this has gone on too long, we must not allow it. An excursion to Holterhof— for the four of us! And we will make it within the next few days! It is so beautiful now, the season is so enchanting and the barometer is steady. The buds will be opening in the park, it may well be pleasanter in its spring array than in the heat of summer, when Anna and I went walking there. Suddenly I feel a positive nostalgia

for the black swans which—you remember, Anna—glided over the moats in such melancholy pride with their red bills and oar-feet. How they disguised their appetite in condescension when we fed them! We must take along some bread for them. . . . Let's see, today is Friday—we will go Sunday, is that settled? Only Sunday would do for Eduard, and for Mr. Keaton too, I imagine. Of course there will be a crowd out on Sunday, but that means nothing to me, I like mixing with people in their Sunday best, I share in their enjoyment, I like being where there's 'something doing'—at the outdoor carnivals at Oberkassel, when it smells of fried food and the children are licking away at red sugar-sticks and, in front of the circus tent, such fantastically vulgar people are tinkling and tootling and shouting. I find it marvellous. Anna thinks otherwise. She finds it sad. Yes, you do, Anna—and you prefer the aristocratic sadness of the pair of black swans in the moat. . . . I have an inspiration, children —we'll go by water! The trip by land on the street railway is simply boring. Not a scrap of woods and hardly an open field. It's much more amusing by water, Father Rhine shall convey us. Eduard, will you see to getting a steamship schedule? Or, just a moment, if we want to be really luxurious, we'll indulge ourselves and hire a private motorboat for the trip up the Rhine. Then we'll be quite by ourselves, like the black swans. . . . All that remains to be settled is whether we want to set sail in the morning or the afternoon."

The consensus was in favour of the morning. Eduard thought that, in any case, he had heard that the castle was open to visitors only into the early hours of the afternoon. It should be Sunday morning, then. Under Rosalie's energetic urging, the arrangements were soon made and agreed on. It was Keaton who was designated to charter the motorboat. They would meet again at the point of departure, the Rathaus quay, by the Water-gauge Clock, the day after tomorrow at nine.

And so they did. It was a sunny and rather windy morning. The quay was jammed with a crowd of pushing people who, with their children and their bicycles, were waiting to go aboard one of the white steamers of the Cologne-Düsseldorf Navigation Company. The chartered motorboat lay ready for the Tümmlers and their companion. Its master, a man with rings in his ear-lobes, clean-shaven upper lip, and a reddish mariner's beard under his chin, helped the ladies aboard. The party had hardly seated themselves on the curved bench under the awning, which was supported by stanchions, before he got under way. The boat made good time against the current of the broad river, whose banks, incidentally, were utterly prosaic. The old castle tower, the crooked tower of the Lambertuskirche, the harbour installations, were left behind. More of the same sort of thing appeared beyond the next bend in the river—warehouses, factory buildings. Little by little, behind the stone jetties which extended from the shore into the river, the country became more rural. Hamlets, old fishing villages—whose names Eduard, and Keaton too, knew—lay, protected by dikes, before a flat landscape of meadows, fields, willow-bushes, and pools. So it would be, however many windings the river made, for a good hour

and a half, until they reached their destination.
But how right they had been, Rosalie exclaimed,
to decide on the boat instead of covering the distance in a fraction of the time by the horrible
route through the suburbs! She seemed to be
heartily enjoying the elemental charm of the
journey by water. Her eyes closed, she sang a
snatch of some happy tune into the wind, which
at moments was almost stormy: "O water-wind,
I love thee; lovest thou me, O water-wind?" Her
face, which had grown thinner, looked very ap-
pealing under the little felt hat with the feather,
and the grey-and-red-checked coat she had on—
of light woollen material with a turn-down collar
—was very becoming to her. Anna and Eduard
had also worn coats for the voyage, and only
Keaton, who sat between mother and daughter,
contented himself with a grey sweater under his
tweed jacket. His handkerchief hung out, and,
suddenly opening her eyes and turning, Rosalie
stuffed it deep into his breast pocket.

"Propriety, propriety, young man!" she said,
shaking her head in decorous reproof.

He smiled: "Thank you," and then wanted to

know what song it was she had just been singing.

"Song?" she asked. "Was I singing? That was
only singsong, not a song." And she closed her
eyes again and hummed, her lips scarcely moving: "How I love thee, O water-wind!"

Then she began chattering through the noise
of the motor, and—often having to hold on to her
hat, which the wind was trying to tear from her
still abundant, wavy grey hair—expatiated on
how it would be possible to extend the Rhine
trip beyond Holterhof, to Leverkusen and Cologne, and from there on past Bonn to Godesberg
and Bad Honnef at the foot of the Siebengebirge.
It was beautiful there, the trim watering-place on
the Rhine, amid vineyards and orchards, and it
had an alkaline mineral spring that was very
good for rheumatism. Anna looked at her; she
knew that her mother now suffered intermit-
tently from lumbago, and had once or twice considered going to Godesberg or Honnef with her
in the early summer, to take the waters. There
was something almost involuntary in the way
she chattered on about the beneficial spring,

catching her breath as she spoke into the wind;
it made Anna think that her mother was even
now not free from the shooting pains that char-
acterize the disease.

After an hour they breakfasted on a few ham
sandwiches and washed them down with port
from little travelling-cups. It was half past eleven
when the boat made fast to a flimsy dock, inade-
quate for larger vessels, which was built out into
the river near the castle and the park. Rosalie
paid off the boatman, as they had decided that it
would after all be easier to make the return journey by land, on the street railway. The park did
not extend quite to the river. They had to follow
a rather damp footpath across a meadow, before
a venerable, seigniorial landscape, well cared for
and well clipped, received them. From an ele-
vated circular terrace, with benches in yew ar-
bours, avenues of magnificent trees, most of them
already in bud, though many shoots were still
hidden under their shiny brown covers, led in
various directions—finely gravelled promenades,
often arched over by meeting branches, between
rows, and sometimes double rows, of beeches,

yews, lindens, horse chestnuts, tall elms. Rare
and curious trees, brought from distant countries,
were also to be seen, planted singly on stretches
of lawn—strange conifers, fern-leafed beeches,
and Keaton recognized the Californian sequoia
and the swamp cypress with its supplementary
breathing-roots.

Rosalie took no interest in these curiosities.
Nature, she considered, must be familiar, or it
did not speak to the heart. But the beauty of the
park did not seem to hold much charm for her.
Scarcely glancing up now and again at the proud
tree-trunks, she walked silently on, with Eduard
at her side, behind his young tutor and the hob-
bling Anna—who, however, soon hit on a ma-
nœuvre to change the arrangement. She stopped
and summoned her brother to tell her the names
of the avenue they were following and of the
winding footpath that crossed it just there. For
all these paths and avenues had old, traditional
names, such as "Fan Avenue," "Trumpet Avenue," and so on. Then, as they moved on, Anna
kept Eduard beside her and left Ken behind with
Rosalie. He carried her coat, which she had taken

off, for not a breath of wind stirred in the park and it was much warmer than it had been on the water. The spring sun shone gently through the high branches, dappled the roads, and played on the faces of the four, making them blink. In her finely tailored brown suit, which closely sheathed her slight, youthful figure, Frau von Tümmler walked at Ken's side, now and again casting a veiled, smiling look at her coat as it hung over his arm. "There they are!" she cried, and pointed to the pair of black swans; for they were now walking along the poplar-bordered moat, and the birds, aware of the approaching visitors, were gliding nearer, at a stately pace, across the slightly scummy water. "How beautiful they are! Anna, do you recognize them? How majestically they carry their necks! Where is the bread for them?" Keaton pulled it out of his pocket, wrapped in newspaper, and handed it to her. It was warm from his body, and she took some of the bread and began to eat it.

"But it's stale and hard," he cried, with a gesture that came too late to stop her.

"I have good teeth," she answered.

One of the swans, however, pushing close against the bank, spread its dark wings and beat the air with them, stretching out its neck and hissing angrily up at her. They laughed at its jealousy, but at the same time felt a little afraid. Then the birds received their rightful due. Rosalie threw them the stale bread, piece after piece, and, swimming slowly back and forth, they accepted it with imperturbable dignity.

"Yet I fear," said Anna as they walked on, "that the old devil won't soon forget your robbing him of his food. He displayed a well-bred pique the whole time."

"Not at all," answered Rosalie. "He was only afraid for a moment that I would eat it all and leave none for him. After that, he must have relished it all the more, since I relished it."

They came to the castle, to the smooth circular pond which mirrored it and in which, to one side, lay a miniature island bearing a solitary poplar. On the expanse of gravel before the flight of steps leading to the gracefully winged structure, whose considerable dimensions its extreme daintiness seemed to efface, and whose pink façade was crumbling a little, stood a number of people who, as they waited for the eleven-o'clock conducted tour, were passing the time by examining the armorial pediment with its figures, the clock, heedless of time and supported by an angel, which surmounted it, the stone wreaths above the tall white portals, and comparing them with the descriptions in their guidebooks. Our friends joined them, and, like them, looked at the charmingly decorated feudal architecture, up to the *œils-de-bœuf* in the slate-coloured garret storey. Figures clad with mythological scantness, Pan and his nymphs, stood on pedestals beside the long windows, flaking away like the four sandstone lions which, with sullen expressions, their paws crossed, flanked the steps and the ramp.

Keaton was enthusiastic over so much history. He found everything "splendid" and "excitingly Continental." Oh dear, to think of his own prosaic country across the Atlantic! There was none of this sort of crumbling aristocratic grace over there, for there had been no Electors and Landgraves, able, in absolute sovereignty, to indulge their passion for magnificence, to their own honour and to the honour of culture. However, his attitude toward the culture which, in its dignity, had not moved on with time, was not so reverent but that, to the amusement of the waiting crowd, he impudently seated himself astride the back of one of the sentinel lions, though it was equipped with a sharp spike, like certain toy horses whose rider can be removed. He clasped the spike in front of him with both hands, pretended, with cries of "Hi!" and "Giddap!" that he was giving the beast the spurs, and really could not have presented a more attractive picture of youthful high spirits. Anna and Eduard avoided looking at their mother.

Then bolts creaked, and Keaton hastened to dismount from his steed, for the caretaker, a man wearing military breeches and with his left sleeve empty and rolled up—to all appearance a retired non-commissioned officer whose service injury had been compensated by this quiet post—swung open the central portal and admitted the visitors. He stationed himself in the lofty doorway and, letting them file past him, not only distributed entrance tickets from a small pad, but managed

too, with his one hand, to tear them half across.
Meanwhile, he had already begun to talk; speaking out of his crooked mouth in a hoarse, gravelly voice, he rattled off the information which he had learned by rote and repeated a thousand times: that the sculptured decoration on the façade was by an artist whom the Elector had summoned for the purpose from Rome; that the castle and the park were the work of a French architect; and that the structure was the most important example of Rococo on the Rhine, though it exhibited traces of the transition to the Louis Seize style; that the castle contained fifty-five rooms and had cost eight hundred thousand taler—and so on.

The vestibule exhaled a musty chill. Here, standing ready in rows, were large boat-shaped felt slippers, into which, amid much snickering from the ladies, the party were obliged to step for the protection of the precious parquets, which were, indeed, almost the chief objects of interest in the apartments dedicated to pleasure, through which, awkwardly shuffling and sliding, the party followed their droning one-armed guide. Of different patterns in the various rooms, the central intarsias represented all sorts of star shapes and floral fantasies. Their gleaming surfaces received the reflections of the visitors, of the cambered state furniture, while tall mirrors, set between gilded pillars wreathed in garlands and tapestry fields of flowered silk framed in gilded listels, repeatedly interchanged the images of the crystal chandeliers, the amorous ceiling paintings, the medallions and emblems of the hunt and music over the doors, and, despite a great many blind-spots, still succeeded in evoking the illusion of rooms opening into one another as far as the eye could see. Unbridled luxuriousness, unqualified insistence on gratification, were to be read in the cascades of elegant ornamentation, of gilded scrollwork, to which only the inviolable style and taste of the period that had produced them set bounds. In the round banquet room, around which, in niches, stood Apollo and the Muses, the inlaid woodwork of the floor gave place to marble, like that which sheathed the walls. Rosy *putti* drew back a painted drapery from the pierced cupola, through which the daylight fell, and from the galleries, as the caretaker said, music had once floated down to the banqueters below.

Ken Keaton was walking beside Frau von Tümmler, with his hand under her elbow. Every American takes his lady across the street in this fashion. Separated from Anna and Eduard, among strangers, they followed close behind the caretaker, who hoarsely, in wooden book phrases, unreeled his text and told the party what they were seeing. They were not, he informed them, seeing everything that was to be seen. Of the castle's fifty-five rooms, he went on—and, following his routine, dropped for a moment into vapid insinuation, though his face, with its crooked mouth, remained wholly aloof from the playfulness of his words—not all were simply open without further ado. The gentry of those days had a great taste for jokes and secrets and mysteries, for hiding-places in the background, retreats that, offering opportunities, were accessible through mechanical tricks—such as this one here, for example. And he stopped beside a pier glass, which, in response to his pressing upon a spring, slid aside, surprising the sightseers by a view of a narrow circular staircase with delicately latticed banisters. Immediately to the left, on a pedestal at its foot, stood an armless three-quarters torso of a man with a wreath of berries in his hair and kirtled with a spurious festoon of leaves; leaning back a little, he smiled down into space over his goat's beard, priapic and welcoming. There were ah's and oh's. "And so on," said the guide, as he said each time, and returned the trick mirror to its place. "And so too," he said, walking on; and made a tapestry panel, which had nothing to distinguish it from the others, open as a secret door and disclose a passageway leading into darkness and exhaling an odor of mould. "That's the sort of thing they liked," said the one-armed caretaker. "Other times, other manners," he added, with sententious stupidity, and continued the tour.

The felt boats were not easy to keep on one's feet. Frau von Tümmler lost one of hers; it slid some distance away over the smooth floor, and while Keaton laughingly retrieved it and, kneeling, put it on her foot again, they were overtaken by the party of sightseers. Again he put his hand under her elbow, but, with a dreamy smile, she remained standing where she was, looking after the party as it disappeared into further rooms; then, still supported by his hand, she turned and hurriedly ran her fingers over the tapestry, where it had opened.

"You aren't doing it right," he whispered. "Let me. It was here." He found the spring, the door responded, and the mouldy air of the secret passageway enveloped them as they advanced a few steps. It was dark around them. With a sigh drawn from the uttermost depths of her being, Rosalie flung her arms around the young man's neck; and he too happily embraced her trembling form. "Ken, Ken," she stammered, her face against his throat, "I love you, I love you, and you know it, I haven't been able to hide it from you completely, and you, and you, do you love me too, a little, only a little, tell me, can you love me with your youth, as Nature has bestowed it on me to love you in my grey age? Yes? Yes? Your mouth then, oh, at last, your young mouth, for which I have hungered, your dear lips, like this, like this— Can I kiss? Tell me, can I, my sweet awakener? I can do everything, as you can. Ken, love is strong, a miracle, so it comes and works great miracles. Kiss me, darling! I have hungered for your lips, oh how much, for I must tell you that my poor head slipped into all sorts of sophistries, like thinking that broad-mindedness and libertinism were not for me, and that the contradiction between my way of life and my innate convictions threatened to destroy me. Oh, Ken, it was the sophistries that almost destroyed me, and my hunger for you. . . . It is you, it is you at last, this is your hair, this is your mouth, this breath comes from your nostrils, the arms that I know are around me, this is your body's warmth, that I relished and the swan was angry. . . ."

A little more, and she would have sunk to the ground before him. But he held her, and drew her along the passage, which grew a little lighter. Steps descended to the open round arch of a door, behind which murky light fell from above on an alcove whose tapestries were worked with billing pairs of doves. In the alcove stood a sort of causeuse, beside which a carved Cupid with blindfolded eyes held a thing like a torch. There, in the musty dampness, they sat down.

"Ugh, it smells of death," Rosalie shuddered against his shoulder. "How sad, Ken my darling, that we have to be here amid this decay. It was in kind Nature's lap, fanned by her airs, in the sweet breath of jasmines and alders, that I dreamed it should be, it was there that I should have kissed you for the first time, and not in this grave! Go away, stop it, you devil, I will be yours, but not in this mould. I will come to you tomorrow, in your room, tomorrow morning, perhaps even tonight. I'll arrange it, I'll play a trick on my would-be-wise Anna. . . ." He made her promise. And indeed they felt too that they must rejoin the others, either by going on or by retracing their steps. Keaton decided in favour of going on. They left the dead pleasure chamber by another door, again there was a dark passageway, it turned, mounted, and they came to a rusty gate, which, in response to Ken's strenuous pushing and tugging, shakily gave way and which was so overgrown outside with leathery

vines and creepers that they could hardly force
their way through. The open air received them.
There was a plash of waters; cascades flowed
down behind broad beds set with flowers of the
early year, yellow narcissuses. It was the back
garden of the castle. The group of visitors was
just approaching from the right; the caretaker
had left them; Anna and her brother were bringing up the rear. The pair mingled with the fore-
most, who were beginning to scatter toward the
fountains and in the direction of the wooded
park. It was natural to stand there, look around,
and go to meet the brother and sister. "Where
in the world have you been?" And: "That's just
what we want to ask *you*!" And: "How could
we possibly lose sight of one another so?" Anna
and Eduard had even, they said, turned back to
look for the lost couple, but in vain. "After all,
you couldn't have vanished from the face of the
earth," said Anna. "No more than you," Rosalie
answered. None of them looked at the others.

Walking between rhododendrons, they circled
the wing of the castle and arrived at the pond in
front of it, which was quite close to the street-

railway stop. If the boat trip upstream, following the windings of the Rhine, had been long, the return journey on the tram, speeding noisily through industrial districts and past colonies of workmen's houses, was correspondingly swift. The brother and sister now and again exchanged a word with each other or with their mother, whose hand Anna held for a while because she had seen her trembling. The party broke up in the city, near the Königsallee.

§~

Frau von Tümmler did not go to Ken Keaton. That night, toward morning, a severe indisposition attacked her and alarmed the household. What, on its first return, had made her so proud, so happy, what she had extolled as a miracle of Nature and the sublime work of feeling, reappeared calamitously. She had had the strength to ring, but when her daughter and the maid came hurrying in, they found her lying in a faint in her blood.

The physician, Dr. Oberloskamp, was soon on the spot. Reviving under his ministrations, she appeared astonished at his presence.

"What, Doctor, you here?" she said. "I suppose Anna must have troubled you to come? But it is only 'after the manner of women' with me."

"At times, my dear Frau von Tümmler, these functions require a certain supervision," the grey-haired doctor answered. To her daughter he declared categorically that the patient must be brought, preferably by ambulance, to the gynæcological hospital. The case demanded the most thorough examination—which, he added, might show that it was not dangerous. Certainly, the metrorrhagias—the first one, of which he had only now heard, and this alarming recurrence—might well be caused by a myoma, which could easily be removed by an operation. In the hands of the director and chief surgeon of the hospital, Professor Muthesius, her dear mother would receive the most trustworthy care.

His recommendations were followed—without resistance on Frau von Tümmler's part, to Anna's silent amazement. Through it all, her mother only stared into the distance with her eyes very wide open.

The bimanual examination, performed by Muthesius, revealed a uterus far too large for the patient's age, abnormally thickened tissue in the
tube, and, instead of an ovary already greatly reduced in size, a huge tumour. The curettage
showed carcinoma cells, some of them character-
istically ovarian; but others left no doubt that
cancer cells were entering into full development
in the uterus itself. All the malignancy showed
signs of rapid growth.

The professor, a man with a double chin, a
very red complexion, and water-blue eyes into
which tears came easily—their presence having
nothing whatever to do with the state of his emotions—raised his head from the microscope.

"Condition extensive, if you ask me," he said
to his assistant, whose name was Dr. Knepperges.
"However, we will operate, Knepperges. Total
extirpation, down to the last connective tissue in
the true pelvis and to all lymphatic tissue, can in
any case prolong life."

But the picture that the opening of the abdominal cavity revealed, in the white light of the

arc-lamps, to the doctors and nurses, was too terrible to permit any hope even of a temporary improvement. The time for that was long since past. Not only were all the pelvic organs already involved; the peritoneum too showed, to the naked eye alone, the murderous cell groups, all the glands of the lymphatic system were carcinomatously thickened, and there was no doubt that there were also foci of cancer cells in the liver.

"Just take a look at this mess, Knepperges," said Muthesius. "Presumably it exceeds your expectations." That it also exceeded his own, he gave no sign. "Ours is a noble art," he added, his eyes filling with tears that meant nothing, "but this is expecting a little too much of it. We can't cut all that away. If you think that you observe metastasis in both ureters, you observe correctly. Uremia cannot but soon set in. Mind you, I don't deny that the uterus itself is producing the voracious brood. Yet I advise you to adopt my opinion, which is that the whole story started from the ovary—that is, from immature ovarian cells which often remain there from birth and which, after the menopause, through heaven knows what process of stimulation, begin to develop malignantly. And then the organism, *post festum*, if you like, is shot through, drenched, inundated, with estrogen hormones, which leads to hormonal hyperplasia of the uteral mucous membrane, with concomitant hemorrhages."

Knepperges, a thin, ambitiously conceited man, made a brief, covertly ironical bow of thanks for the lecture.

"Well, let's get on with it, *ut aliquid fieri videatur*," said the professor. "We must leave her what is essential for life, however steeped in melancholy the word is in this instance."

Anna was waiting upstairs in the hospital room when her mother, who had been brought up by the elevator, returned on her stretcher and was put to bed by the nurses. During the process she awoke from her post-narcotic sleep and said indistinctly:

"Anna, my child, he hissed at me."

"Who, dearest Mama?"

"The black swan."

She was already asleep again. But she often remembered the swan during the next few weeks, his blood-red bill, the black beating of his wings. Her suffering was brief. Uremic coma soon plunged her into profound unconsciousness, and, double pneumonia developing, her exhausted heart could only hold out for a matter of days.

Just before the end, when it was but a few hours away, her mind cleared again. She raised her eyes to her daughter, who sat at her bedside, holding her hand.

"Anna," she said, and was able to push the upper part of her body a little toward the edge of the bed, closer to her confidante, "do you hear me?"

"Certainly I hear you, dear, dear Mama."

"Anna, never say that Nature deceived me, that she is sardonic and cruel. Do not rail at her, as I do not. I am loth to go away—from you all, from life with its spring. But how should there be spring without death? Indeed, death is a great instrument of life, and if for me it borrowed the guise of resurrection, of the joy of love, that was not a lie, but goodness and mercy."

Another little push, closer to her daughter, and a failing whisper:

"Nature—I have always loved her, and she—has been loving to her child."

Rosalie died a gentle death, regretted by all who knew her.

The Principal Works of Thomas Mann

First Editions in German

DER KLEINE HERR FRIEDEMANN
[Little Herr Friedemann]. Tales
Berlin, S. Fischer Verlag. 1898

BUDDENBROOKS
Novel
Berlin, S. Fischer Verlag. 1901

TRISTAN
Contains *Tonio Kröger*. Tales   *Berlin, S. Fischer Verlag.* 1903

FIORENZA
Drama   *Berlin, S. Fischer Verlag.* 1905

KÖNIGLICHE HOHEIT
[Royal Highness]. Novel   *Berlin, S. Fischer Verlag.* 1909

DER TOD IN VENEDIG
[Death in Venice]. Short novel   *Berlin, S. Fischer Verlag.* 1913

DAS WUNDERKIND
[The Infant Prodigy]. Tales   *Berlin, S. Fischer Verlag.* 1914

BETRACHTUNGEN EINES UNPOLITISCHEN
Autobiographical reflections   *Berlin, S. Fischer Verlag.* 1918

HERR UND HUND
[A Man and His Dog]. Idyll
Contains also *Gesang vom Kindchen,* an idyll in verse
Berlin, S. Fischer Verlag. 1919

WÄLSUNGENBLUT
Tale   *München, Phantasus Verlag.* 1921

BEKENNTNISSE DES HOCHSTAPLERS FELIX KRULL
Fragment of a novel   *Stuttgart, Deutsche Verlags-Anstalt.*

BEMÜHUNGEN
Essays   *Berlin, S. Fischer Verlag.* 1922

REDE UND ANTWORT
  Essays   *Berlin, S. Fischer Verlag.*   1922

DER ZAUBERBERG
  [The Magic Mountain]. Novel   *Berlin, S. Fischer Verlag.*   1924

UNORDNUNG UND FRÜHES LEID
  [Disorder and Early Sorrow]. Short novel
                                          Berlin, S. Fischer Verlag.   1926
KINO
  Fragment of a novel   *Berlin, S. Fischer Verlag.*   1926

PARISER RECHENSCHAFT
  Travelogue   *Berlin, S. Fischer Verlag.*   1926

DEUTSCHE ANSPRACHE
  Ein Appell an die Vernunft   *Berlin, S. Fischer Verlag.*   1930

DIE FORDERUNG DES TAGES
  Essays   *Berlin, S. Fischer Verlag.*   1930

MARIO UND DER ZAUBERER
  [Mario and the Magician]. Short novel
                                          Berlin, S. Fischer Verlag.   1930
GOETHE ALS REPRÄSENTANT DES
    BÜRGERLICHEN ZEITALTERS
  Lecture   *Berlin, S. Fischer Verlag.*   1932

JOSEPH UND SEINE BRÜDER
  [Joseph and His Brothers]. Novel
  I. Die Geschichten Jaakobs. 1933.
  II. Der junge Joseph. 1934.
  III. Joseph in Ägypten. 1936.
  IV. Joseph, der Ernährer. 1943.
                    I, II, Berlin, S. Fischer Verlag.
                    III, Vienna, Bermann-Fischer Verlag.
                    IV, Stockholm, Bermann-Fischer Verlag.

LEIDEN UND GRÖSSE DER MEISTER
  Essays   *Berlin, S. Fischer Verlag.*   1935

FREUD UND DIE ZUKUNFT
  Lecture   *Vienna, Bermann-Fischer Verlag.*   1936

EIN BRIEFWECHSEL
  [An Exchange of Letters]
                          Zürich, Dr. Oprecht & Helbling AG.   1937

DAS PROBLEM DER FREIHEIT
    Essay   *Stockholm, Bermann-Fischer Verlag.*

SCHOPENHAUER
    Essay   *Stockholm, Bermann-Fischer Verlag.*

ACHTUNG, EUROPA!
    Manifesto   *Stockholm, Bermann-Fischer Verlag.*

DIE SCHÖNSTEN ERZÄHLUNGEN
    Contains *Tonio Kröger, Der Tod in Venedig, Unordnung*
    und frühes Leid, Mario und der Zauberer
                     Stockholm, Bermann-Fischer Verlag.   1938

LOTTE IN WEIMAR
    [The Beloved Returns]. Novel
                     Stockholm, Bermann-Fischer Verlag.   1939

DIE VERTAUSCHTEN KÖPFE
    Eine indische Legende [The Transposed Heads]
                     Stockholm, Bermann-Fischer Verlag.   1940

DEUTSCHE HÖRER
    [Listen, Germany!] Broadcasts
                     Stockholm, Bermann-Fischer Verlag.   1942

DAS GESETZ
    [The Tables of the Law]
                     Stockholm, Bermann-Fischer Verlag.   1944

DOKTOR FAUSTUS: DAS LEBEN DES DEUTSCHEN TONSETZERS
    ADRIAN LEVERKÜHN, ERZÄHLT VON EINEM FREUNDE
    Novel   *Stockholm, Bermann-Fischer Verlag.*   1947

DER ERWÄHLTE
    [The Holy Sinner]. Novel
                     Frankfurt am Main, S. Fischer Verlag.   1951

DIE BETROGENE
    [The Black Swan]. Short Novel
                     Frankfurt am Main, S. Fischer Verlag.   1953

American Editions in Translation
published by ALFRED A. KNOPF, *New York*

ROYAL HIGHNESS: A NOVEL OF GERMAN COURT LIFE
    Translated by A. Cecil Curtis   1916

---

* Included in *Stories of Three Decades*, translated by H. T. Lowe-
Porter.

STORIES OF THREE DECADES
  *Translated by H. T. Lowe-Porter. Contains all of Thomas
  Mann's fiction prior to 1940 except the long novels*   1936

AN EXCHANGE OF LETTERS
  Translated by H. T. Lowe-Porter †   1937

FREUD, GOETHE, WAGNER
  *Translated by H. T. Lowe-Porter and Rita Matthias-
  Reil. Three essays*   1937

THE COMING VICTORY OF DEMOCRACY
  Translated by Agnes E. Meyer †   1938

THIS PEACE
  Translated by H. T. Lowe-Porter †   1938

THIS WAR
  Translated by Eric Sutton †   1940

THE BELOVED RETURNS
  [Lotte in Weimar]
  Translated by H. T. Lowe-Porter   1940

THE TRANSPOSED HEADS
  Translated by H. T. Lowe-Porter   1941

ORDER OF THE DAY
  Political Essays and Speeches of Two Decades
  *Translated by H. T. Lowe-Porter, Agnes E. Meyer, and
  Eric Sutton*   1942

LISTEN, GERMANY!
  Twenty-five Radio Messages to the German People over
  BBC   1943

THE TABLES OF THE LAW
  Translated by H. T. Lowe-Porter   1945

ESSAYS OF THREE DECADES
  Translated by H. T. Lowe-Porter   1947

DOCTOR FAUSTUS: THE LIFE OF THE GERMAN COMPOSER ADRIAN
  LEVERKÜHN AS TOLD BY A FRIEND
  Translated by H. T. Lowe-Porter   1948

THE HOLY SINNER
  Translated by H. T. Lowe-Porter   1951

THE BLACK SWAN
  Translated by Willard R. Trask   1954

---

† Also included in *Order of the Day.*

PRINTER'S NOTE

This book was set on the Linotype in Janson, a recutting made direct from type cast in matrices made by Anton Janson some time between 1660 and 1687. This type is an excellent example of the influential and singularly sturdy Dutch types that prevailed in England prior to Caslon. It was from the Dutch types that Caslon developed his own incomparable designs.

The book was composed by The Plimpton Press, Norwood, Massachusetts. Printed and bound by The Book Press, Brattleboro, Vt. The typography and binding design are by W. A. Dwiggins.